camp CONFIDENTIAL

Second Summer

WISH YOU WEREN'T HERE

GROSSET & DUNLAP
Published by the Penguin Group
Penguin Group (USA) Inc., 375 Hudson Street,
New York, New York 10014, U.S.A.
Penguin Group (Canada), 90 Eglinton Avenue East, Suite 700,
Toronto, Ontario, Canada M4P 2Y3 (a division of Pearson Penguin Canada Inc.)
Penguin Books Ltd, 80 Strand, London WC2R 0RL, England
Penguin Ireland, 25 St Stephen's Green,
Dublin 2, Ireland (a division of Penguin Books Ltd)
Penguin Group (Australia), 250 Camberwell Road, Camberwell,
Victoria 3124, Australia (a division of Pearson Australia Group Pty Ltd)
Penguin Books India Pvt Ltd, 11 Community Centre, Panchsheel Park,
New Delhi - 110 017, India
Penguin Group (NZ), Cnr Airborne and Rosedale Roads,
Albany, Auckland 1310, New Zealand (a division of Pearson New Zealand Ltd)
Penguin Books (South Africa) (Pty) Ltd, 24 Sturdee Avenue, Rosebank,
Johannesburg 2196, South Africa

Penguin Books Ltd, Registered Offices:
80 Strand, London WC2R 0RL, England

Cover designed by Ching N. Chan. Interiors designed by Rosanne Guararra.
Front cover image © Photodisc Photography/Getty Images/Veer Incorporated.
Text copyright © 2006 by Grosset & Dunlap. All rights reserved. Published
by Grosset & Dunlap, a division of Penguin Young Readers Group, 345 Hudson
Street, New York, New York 10014. GROSSET & DUNLAP is a trademark of
Penguin Group (USA) Inc. Printed in the U.S.A.

Library of Congress Control Number: 2005033183

ISBN 0-448-44266-3   10 9 8 7 6 5 4 3 2

camp CONFIDENTIAL

Second Summer

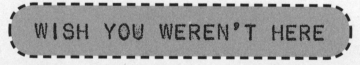

WISH YOU WEREN'T HERE

by Melissa J. Morgan

Grosset & Dunlap

chapter ONE

Hey, Diane!

I was so glad to get your letter yesterday. You have no idea. And thanks for sending the books—I've never read <u>The Phantom Tollbooth</u> or <u>Elsewhere</u>, but if they're as great as you say, I'm sure I'll love them! I've finished up all the assigned summer reading, too, so I've been looking for a new book. I can't believe we're going to be eighth-graders next year! That makes us practically high schoolers! Can you believe it?? I feel like we were just in Mrs. Underhill's first-grade class, learning how to sound out words and yelling at the boys for calling her Mrs. Underwear!

So how are things back home? Have you been hanging out with Taylor a lot? Are you and your family still going up to Lake Winnipesaukee this year? I never thought I'd say it, but I've been thinking about home a lot lately. It's not that I don't <u>love</u> being back at Camp Lakeview—I do. But so much has changed this year. Like I wrote you, they split up all the girls who were in my bunk last year, 3C. It's not so bad—we still all hang out together, and some of the new girls are pretty cool—but I still miss having everyone together.

And then, well—can you <u>believe</u> who showed up at camp this year? Maybe that's why I can't stop thinking about home—this year, "home" has come to camp. You'd think it would be nice having a girl from back home here at camp. We could tell stories about home, introduce each other to our new friends, and hang out. Instead it's just . . . I dunno . . . <u>awkward!</u> I try to be nice, but I really get the feeling she doesn't want to hang out with me, like I'm not popular enough or something. But this is <u>camp</u>, not school! ARRRGGH! It's so frustrating. Everyone thinks we should be best buddies because we're from the same town, but I think she'd rather eat bugs than be my friend. I don't know why. I've always thought she was sorta cool . . .

"Sarah?"

At the sound of her name, Sarah felt herself jump about three feet in the air. As soon as she looked down at the person calling her, she felt her face flush bright red. She knew there was no way that Abby could have known she was writing about her, but she still felt funny. She and Abby weren't friends, exactly, but they'd never out-and-out fought, either. Pasting a big smile on her face, Sarah shoved the unfinished letter into the envelope and stood up from the low tree branch she was sitting on.

"Yeah?"

Abby pulled her long brown hair out of its pony-tail and piled it in a messy knot at the back of her neck. "Becky wants us all back inside the cabin," she explained, not quite looking Sarah in the eye. "She sent me out here to get you. They're telling us what free-choice activities we got this session."

Sarah felt her smile turn into a real one at that news, even though Abby turned around and started walking back to the cabin without even waiting for her to catch up. *Activities,* she thought. *Meaning hopefully, by this time tomorrow, Alex, Brynn, Valerie, and I will all be in sports together again. Awesome!*

Even though camp had only been in session for two weeks, Sarah felt like she might lose it completely if she didn't get to take part in some athletic activity very soon. Each session, each of the campers was assigned two elective "activities," and Sarah *always* signed up for sports—along with Alex, Brynn, Valerie, and a bunch of their other friends from 3C. Last session, though, Sarah ended up getting photography and nature. And while she'd enjoyed them both, she felt like a piece of her body was missing. She *needed* to play sports. And this year—with Abby McDougal, Jock Extraordinaire from Sarah's very own middle school, not only at Camp Lakeview but in the same bunk as Sarah—she felt like she had a lot to prove.

Sarah ran to catch up with Abby, still wearing her big smile. Abby looked a little surprised, like she hadn't expected Sarah to smile at her. "So . . ." Abby said awkwardly, "what did you sign up for?"

"Sports," Sarah replied. "And something else. I

don't remember. Sports is the most important."

"Really?" asked Abby. If she'd looked surprised before, now she looked shocked. "I didn't think you were that great an athlete. I thought you would have signed up for, I don't know—*newspaper* or something."

Sarah cringed. Abby said "newspaper" like it was the lamest thing imaginable. Abby was about the best female athlete at Winthrop Middle School, and, since sports were really important in Winthrop, that made her one of the popular kids. Sarah didn't play sports at school, and was *not* one of the popular kids. She felt like Abby was trying to tell her she wasn't *cool* enough to play sports.

"*Actually,*" Sarah replied, "I really like playing sports at camp. Me, Alex, Brynn, and Valerie always sign up to play. We all try to be on the same team, and we have an awesome time together. Maybe we'll see you there."

Sarah ran ahead and opened the cabin door, letting it bang behind her. As she entered the cabin, she saw her bunkmates all collected in their bedroom, sitting in small groups on the bottom bunks. Abby followed close behind and went to sit with Gaby, and Alex, Brynn, Valerie, and Grace waved at Sarah and motioned for her to come sit down with them. Sarah shoved her letter into her cubby and scooted over to join her friends.

"Can you believe it's time to switch activities already?" Alex was saying. "I feel like camp just started. Pretty soon it'll be time for the social."

"Ugh, don't remind me," Sarah muttered. She loved almost everything about camp but, having zero interest in boys, couldn't care less about the social.

"Oh, come on," Brynn teased. "You don't know, Sarah. Maybe one of the guys out there has a *mad* crush on you. He'll watch you make the winning goal in sports and then run over and tell you how much he *luuuuuurves* you. . . . At the social, you guys can sit in the corner cuddling and talking about the Red Sox scores or whatever."

Everyone laughed, but Sarah felt her face start to burn. "Well, that's only if I *get* sports this session," she said, quickly changing the subject, "which I really hope I do. Plants are nice, but I can't deal with much more leaf rubbing and algae collecting. No more nature!"

Grace chuckled. "Come on, that was fun. Especially when you fell in the lake."

Sarah snorted, recalling the sample-collection-gone-awry. She'd come out covered in green goo and had to run back to their bunk to change, while Grace tested their sample for pollution. "Yeah, fun for *you*."

At that moment, their counselor, Becky, walked into the room, holding a notebook and followed closely by their counselor-in-training, or CIT, Sophie. "All right, guys!" Becky said with a smile. "Time flies when you're having fun, but here we are two weeks into camp, and it's time to switch activities. Everyone enjoy what you had last time?"

Most of the girls shouted "Yes!" or cheered, but Sarah was a little more subdued. "Sort of," she muttered.

Alex glanced over at her and winked. "We'll all have sports together this time," she whispered. "I can feel it."

Becky looked around at the girls and smiled right at Sarah. "Sarah, you're first up."

Sarah felt her heart start to pound as she got up and followed Becky into the small counselor's bedroom. It wasn't a *scared* excited she felt, it was a *good* excited. The last two weeks had been kind of weird, what with last year's group getting split up, Sarah not getting into sports, and Abby, the biggest jock at Sarah's middle school, suddenly showing up in her bunk. Though she'd been glad to be back at Camp Lakeview, among her camp friends, Sarah had been feeling a little out of place—not the sports star she usually was at camp, not getting to hang with *all* of her friends, and not quite knowing how to approach Abby, who only knew her as quiet, bookish Sarah from back home. But now, everything was about to shift into place. Sarah would be in sports again with all her buddies, and she'd surely impress the pants off Abby with her athletic skills, which would make Abby see how much they had in common and that they should be friends. Just like that, the summer would go from "okay" to "awesome." And Sarah could stop worrying about whether she fit in and just go with the flow, like last year.

"All right, Sarah," Becky said, sitting down and flipping open her notebook. "Good news for you, I think. I know you were bummed not to get sports last time, but just like I promised, I tried extra hard to fit you in this time. So you've got sports and also arts and crafts, babe. You can thank me later—I accept cash, checks, and jelly beans." Becky looked up at Sarah and winked. "Just kidding about the cash and checks. But seriously—jelly beans are always welcome."

Sarah jumped up and whooped. "That's awesome,

Becky! Thank you so much!" She threw her arms around her counselor in a quick hug. "I don't have any jelly beans, but if I come across any, they're yours. Thank you, thank you, thank you."

Becky squeezed Sarah and smiled. "No problem, Sarah. You were a great sport about it last session, no pun intended, and I really appreciate that. So have a great time, and send in Alex next."

"Sure." Sarah felt like she was walking on air back to the other room. It was amazing how fast things could start to look up! She walked back over to her friends and told Alex to head in to Becky.

"So what'd you get?" Alex demanded before leaving.

"Sports and arts and crafts," Sarah replied with a grin.

"All *right*!" Alex patted her on the back as Grace, Valerie, and Brynn all squealed their excitement.

"This session is going to be the *best*," Valerie announced. "Just like old times!"

The four of them chatted about the year before while Alex was gone, and when Alex emerged from the counselor's room and walked over, they pounced on her. "What'd you get, what'd you get?"

Alex shrugged sheepishly. "Nature and newspaper," she replied quietly. She didn't sound as disappointed as Sarah felt, but she didn't sound psyched, either. "Oh well. Looks like algae collection for me. Val, she's ready for you."

Valerie left, and Sarah scooted over to make room for Alex on the bunk. "That stinks, Al," she said softly. "Sports won't be half as much fun without you to compete against."

Alex grinned. "You mean *lose* against," she said. "But think of these two weeks as a practice time. You'll have two weeks to get up to speed, before we go head-to-head in the last session."

Sarah looked up and saw Val walking back from Becky's room. Her small smile gave away nothing.

"*So?*" Sarah asked when Val reached the bunk.

"Photography and ceramics," Val said with a shrug. "Oh well. I guess you'll have to kick butt for all of us, Sars. Grace, you're up next."

As Valerie sat back down and the discussion turned back to the social, Sarah tried to push back the rising panic in her chest. *Okay, so Alex didn't get sports. And neither did Valerie. But that doesn't mean it won't be fun! If all the other 3Cers were in sports with me—even Natalie and Jenna—it would still be fun. It'll still be fun, it'll still be fun, it'll still be fun. . . .*

Grace came back then. "Nature and photography," she said with a sigh. "I don't know what's going on, guys. Why aren't any of us getting sports when it was our first choice?"

"It's weird," Alex agreed. "Poor Sars is going to have to play kickball or whatever with herself."

Grace rolled her eyes. "There *are* other campers besides us in 4C, Al."

"That's right," Candace piped up. "There're plenty of other campers. Like 4A and all the 3-levels and the—"

"All *right*," Alex interrupted. "What I meant was, everyone that *matters* won't be in sports." She gave Sarah a quick wink to let her know she was kidding.

But Sarah felt herself growing quieter and quieter as the conversation went on. *It's true—nobody's in sports*, she thought when Brynn came back and excitedly announced that she'd gotten drama and ceramics. ("Sorry, Sarah," she'd said with a shrug.) *So I get to play sports, but I'll be all alone. Where's the fun in that?*

Gradually, all the other girls in bunk 4C went in to meet with Becky and came back out with either big smiles on their faces or the more surprised looks of not getting what they expected. For the most part, everyone seemed pretty happy—even Sarah's friends, though they hadn't gotten sports, seemed pretty eager to try out the activities they had. To Sarah's amazement, *none* of the other girls came back and announced they'd gotten sports. Between Priya and Tiernan, Becky came back out to the girls' bunks and got everyone's attention. "I'm not done yet, but I heard some grumbling out here." Sarah and her friends exchanged guilty glances. "I know some of you are kind of surprised not be getting your first choice, sports." Sarah looked around the room. About half her bunkmates were nodding in agreement.

"I just wanted to explain that we had way too many girls sign up for sports this session, so we tried to move anyone who'd had it for the last two weeks into their second choice. Hopefully, next session, things will even out a little bit. So buck up, little campers." She grinned and returned to the other room.

"Well, that explains things," Alex said. "Sarah, you're the only one who didn't get sports last time. So you get it this time."

"I guess." Sarah shrugged. She didn't know how to

say that she'd rather not have it at all than have sports without her friends.

As the last girl met with Becky, the rest of 4C started getting ready for dinner. Sarah ran into the bathroom, washed her hands, and splashed some water on her face. As much as she was trying to keep a positive attitude, Sarah couldn't help feeling like her great, everything-in-place summer had just been destroyed. *I'm going to be all alone in sports* and *arts and crafts. How could this get any worse?*

Sarah heard a whoop from the bunks and walked back out with Alex and Brynn. All of her bunkmates were standing in a group by the door, ready to go to dinner.

"So what'd you get, Abby?" Alex asked in a friendly way as they passed Abby and Gaby on their way out the door.

Abby turned to Alex with a big grin. "I'm so psyched! I got nature and *sports!*"

Sarah felt her heart drop into her stomach. She'd been looking forward to being in sports . . . with her friends. Abby had been cold to her since camp started, and every time they spoke it just seemed to emphasize the fact that Sarah wasn't cool enough for Abby. Being in sports alone with her would ratchet the Awkward Meter up from 5 to about 5,000.

I don't believe it, but I think it just got worse.

chapter
TWO

"Okay," Alex was saying as bunk 4C strolled over to the mess hall, "so we won't have many activities together. But the good news is, this time every summer, the counselors start taking volunteers for the social committee!"

Sarah glanced at her friend and sighed. Alex had been coming to Camp Lakeview for years and years, and she always enjoyed sharing all the tips and secrets she'd gained as a Camp Lakeview veteran. Usually Sarah found that part of Alex's personality kind of funny. But in her current mood, it just annoyed her.

"*And?*" she asked. "And that's relevant to the whole activity thing *because . . .*"

Alex glanced back at her and pouted. "Well, if you'd let me *finish*, I'm definitely signing up for this social committee because I want to help make sure this social is the best ever!" Her face brightened as she turned to Brynn and Valerie. "Not that it would be hard to beat last year. Remember that whole animal disaster?"

Sarah couldn't keep herself from smiling.

The year before, the campers had agreed upon a square-dance theme—and Jenna and Chelsea, in some fit of really awful judgment, had thought it would be a funny "prank" to bring real animals from the nature shack into the dance. At the time, it had been awful—the animals had panicked, the campers had freaked out, and mayhem ensued. Looking back on it, though, it seemed kind of funny.

"Anyway," Alex was saying, "I'm definitely signing up."

"Me too!" said Brynn quickly. "I think that's a great idea. And I have all kinds of experience with set decoration and lighting for the stage, so I bet I could really help out with those things."

"Me too!" squealed Valerie. "I mean, I just want to help plan the dance. Maybe make it a little more elegant than last year?"

Everyone chuckled. It would be hard to get less elegant than last year's disaster.

"I think that's a great idea," Grace agreed. "I'll sign up. Maybe Devon will want to go."

Sarah remained silent. She felt her friends all looking back at her, but she didn't say anything. The truth was, she'd rather poke herself in the eye with a sharp stick than spend all that time thinking about a stupid dance. She wanted to get to spend time with her bunkmates, but not *that* way. She'd go crazy listening to them go on and on about boys and who was cuter and who might ask who out . . .

"What do you think, Sars?" Alex asked hopefully. "All four of us on social committee? We'd plan a dance that would keep them talking for years!"

Without looking up from the ground, Sarah shook her head. "I don't think so."

"Why not?" asked Brynn. "I'm telling you, it's going to be *great* this year. And like I said, maybe there's a great sporty guy out there for you—"

"I said *no*, all right? I really don't care about the stupid social." Sarah's friends all stopped short in surprise. Sarah felt her eyes start to burn with tears. *I will not start to cry. I will not start to cry. I will not start to cry.* She'd spent the last two weeks feeling out of place, separated from her best friends, and freaked out that Abby had somehow brought all the stress of Winthrop Middle School to Camp Lakeview. Any day now, Abby might tell her bunkmates how *different* she acted back home—all quiet, a teacher's pet. Not at all jokey or competitive, like she was here. For the most part, Sarah was happy being sort of bookish at home—but camp was her chance to be anyone she wanted to be, away from the watchful eyes of her classmates. When she'd first tried sports, she'd been shocked to discover just how good an athlete she was. Even more surprising was how much fun she had doing it. *But now I'm stuck in sports alone with Abby*, she thought miserably. *I won't get to hang out with my best friends—they'll all be too busy planning the stupid social. Why did I have to be put in bunk 4C?*

She forced her way through her friends without looking any of them in the eye and plodded forward to the mess hall.

"Hey, Sarah! Sarah! Sarah!"

Sarah blinked and looked right toward the sound

of her name. Her friend Jenna, formerly of 3C and now of 4A, was standing on the mess-hall lawn surrounded by a few 4A-ers. She started waving crazily as soon as Sarah looked up, her messy brunette braid flailing as she moved her head to follow Sarah's approach.

"What did you get?" Jenna demanded before Sarah even got all the way up to her.

Sarah sighed. "Sports and arts and crafts."

Jenna's whole face lit up. "Awesome! I'm in sports, too. We're going to kick some boy butt!"

Standing close by, Natalie and Tori laughed. Sarah glanced over and saw that Alyssa and Chelsea were also there.

"I got arts and crafts," Alyssa added. "You and I will definitely have fun in that. I hear we're working with chalk pastels this session."

"Great," Sarah said sarcastically. "The only pastel I can pull off is if I draw a big mud puddle. That's what all of my drawings turn into eventually."

Alyssa laughed. "Oh, you just need to work on your technique a little," she said with a wink. "I'll help you out. And if I ever end up in sports again, heaven forbid, you can teach me how to land a slam dunk."

Sarah smiled. "Deal!"

Right then Justin, one of the boys' counselors, opened the doors to the mess hall and all of the campers started stampeding in. Sarah drifted into the hall with the 4A girls, then split off and went to find the table for 4C. Sarah spotted Brynn and Valerie on the other side of the hall talking to a couple of boys, but Alex was sitting alone at their table, looking around anxiously. As

Sarah approached, her face flooded with relief.

"Sars," she said as Sarah grabbed the chair next to her. "I didn't mean to make you mad with the social-committee stuff. And if you don't want to be on it, you *totally* don't have to. You know that, right?"

Sarah nodded and fiddled with her silverware. "I know."

Alex sighed. "I just . . . you seem upset."

Sarah sighed. She felt her insides turn to mush, the way they always did when she was upset and someone was this nice to her. She knew she'd been mean to snap at Alex. She didn't know how to explain that she was worried about drifting apart from her, Brynn, Val, and Grace, and all this other stuff. Alex seemed so confident all the time—Sarah couldn't imagine her understanding.

"Is it because you're in sports alone?" Alex asked suddenly, looking confused. "I mean, Abby will be in there with you. She seems pretty cool."

Sarah sighed. *There's no way Abby and I will ever be friends, but Alex would never understand that.* "Yeah," she said finally, almost whispering. "I know it's lame. I was worried about being lonely, but yeah, Abby will be there, I guess. It turns out Jenna's in there, too."

Abby, Gaby, and the rest of 4C came over to the table and grabbed seats. Sarah watched them, not wanting to look at Alex and see if she understood. But she felt Alex reach over and pat her shoulder. "You'll kick serious butt without us, Sars," Alex said confidently. "You always do."

Across the table, Gaby grabbed her silverware and looked across the room. "What's for dinner tonight?"

she asked. "I'm starved."

"That's 'cause you barely ate anything at lunch," Alex pointed out.

Gaby shrugged, still craning her neck to see any sign of the CITs with their dinner. "Mac and cheese is bad for you. It's all carbs and fat."

"And *protein*," Abby interjected, unfolding her napkin. "And calcium? Honestly, Gaby, you're lucky you don't play sports. You'd run out of energy in about half a minute with the stuff you eat."

Gaby rolled her eyes. Sarah knew that if anyone else had made that comment, Gaby would have made some nasty retort. But since it was Abby, she'd let it slide.

"Whatever," Gaby muttered, smiling warily. "The point is, I'm hungry."

A few seconds later the CITs began serving the meal, and Sophie came over with a huge tray of meat loaf. "Gross," Gaby whispered as Sophie set it down in the middle of the table. "It looks . . . gray."

"Maybe it came from an old cow," Sarah quipped without thinking. Alex started laughing, and soon most of the table joined in. Even Gaby smiled ruefully as she took a piece of meat loaf and passed the tray around. The only person not laughing was the person who never laughed at Sarah's jokes . . . Abby. She just sat there, stone-faced. It was like Sarah's voice came out on some uncool frequency that Abby couldn't hear.

Nobody else noticed, though. Everyone assumed Sarah and Abby were old friends, since they both came from the same tiny town outside Boston. The truth, though, was that they ran in totally different crowds. Abby hung with the jocks, a bunch of popular girls and boys who sat together at a big lunch table and were all on the Winthrop Middle School sports teams. Sarah had only a few close friends, and they mostly kept to themselves. They were smart enough and well-liked enough by the teachers that some of the kids called them "nerds," but they got along with most everyone. They just weren't *popular*, like Abby and her friends. Sarah frowned as she watched everyone dig in to their meat loaf. She loved coming to camp because she felt as if she could do anything here, and no one could tell her that she wasn't *like* that, that she was too nerdy, not popular enough, whatever. But she felt like Abby was always on the verge of telling her just that.

"Hey," Valerie was saying. "*You* got sports as an activity, right, Abby?"

Abby looked up. "Yeah," she replied. "I can't wait to get out there and play! Why?"

"Well, that means you and Sarah will be in sports together." Val nudged Sarah with her elbow, almost making her spill her bug juice. "See, Sars? You guys will have a *great* time together. Two amazing athletes from the same town! What are the chances?"

Sarah felt her face starting to burn. *She's going to tell everybody. Everyone will know I'm not really a jock.* "Well, I'm not *that* great—"

But Abby was already speaking. "Yeah," she was saying. "Well, actually, I didn't even know Sars *played* sports."

Sarah winced. Sars was a nickname that no one ever called her outside camp. At school, she was just

Sarah—Sarah Peyton, teacher's pet and all-around priss. Well, this was it. Sarah's cover was about to be blown. But she could out herself—she didn't have to wait for Abby to do it.

She put down her bug juice and looked Abby in the eye. "I don't, at home," she said simply.

Alex practically choked on her bug juice. "You *don't?*" she asked, slamming her cup down. "But you're *great*, Sarah! You're like the second-best athlete this camp has ever seen!"

Sarah raised an eyebrow. "*Second* best?"

Alex nodded, smiling. "After me, I mean. Well, maybe *third* best. Jenna's pretty good, too."

"You're *amazing*, is the point," Val chimed in. "You're such a great athlete! So why don't you play on any teams at home? It doesn't make sense."

"Yeah, it's weird," muttered Abby.

Sarah sighed and looked down at her plate. How could she explain it? The truth was, even she wasn't sure why she loved playing sports at camp yet never tried them at home. Was she afraid of losing?

"I guess . . . I'm just really busy at home," Sarah said. She glanced up just in time to see Abby roll her eyes, but she didn't think anyone else saw. "With schoolwork, I mean. And besides, camp is the perfect time to branch out, I think—to try something new." She caught Abby's eye. "With nobody judging you, you know?"

Abby looked away.

"But if you're good at sports, you're good at sports," Alex said, waving around a forkful of green beans. "Why not play on some teams? Don't you think it's a waste, Abby?"

Abby looked up at Alex. "I guess," she said, sounding skeptical, then glanced sideways at Sarah. "If she really *is* good. I've never seen her play."

"She's *amazing*," Grace said, shooting Sarah a big smile.

Abby took a sip of bug juice and shrugged, still unconvinced. "I guess we'll see tomorrow."

Sarah watched Abby as she lost interest in the conversation and went back to her meal. She kind of half-heard her friends turn the conversation, once again, to the social and what they wanted to do on the committee. Sarah guessed she must have looked normal on the outside, because nobody said anything to her, but inside, she was seething. *All right*, she thought. *It's okay that Abby doesn't want to be my friend, or that she thinks she's too cool for me, or whatever. But now she doesn't even believe I'm good at sports! She just doesn't think a "nerd" like me could be good at anything—besides taking tests!*

Sarah was finding it hard to concentrate on her meal. Abby's attitude was making her madder and madder. She poked at her meat loaf and shoved a few bites in her mouth before the CITs came around again to pick up the dinner plates. *I'll show her*, she thought, chewing fiercely. *I'll show her what a "nerd" can do. Tomorrow I'll blow Abby away at sports. If anyone can impress her, I can!*

THREE

In her two years at Camp Lakeview, Sarah had learned that there were two kinds of people: those that got up at the crack of dawn, and those that—well—didn't. Sarah knew she fell into the latter category. She usually had to be dragged out of her bottom bunk, kicking and screaming. But the next day—her first official day back in sports—Sarah was so buzzed, her eyes popped open at the first morning light.

It was the perfect day to show Abby how wrong she'd been. The sun was shining, and there wasn't a cloud in the sky. Feeling totally energized, Sarah took an early shower, put on her favorite cargo shorts and Red Sox hat, and ate everything in sight at breakfast, taking extra pancakes and bacon.

"Hungry much?" asked Gaby, who was picking at her own cornflakes.

Sarah just smiled. "I need all the energy I can get for the first day of sports."

Abby shot her a skeptical look, but Sarah just flashed her sweetest grin. *It doesn't matter what Abby thinks now—I'll show her.*

After breakfast, all the campers split off to attend their first activity.

"Have fun at photography," Sarah told Grace as she headed to the main practice field.

"I will." Grace turned around and flashed Sarah a huge smile. "You have fun in sports, Sarah. Kick some butt for your fellow 4C-ers."

Sarah grinned back. "You know I will."

Sarah practically skipped from the mess hall to the practice field. Now that she had a mission, she felt like she might burst from excitement. Sarah had always been good at "quiet" activities, like reading and schoolwork, and she knew that led some people to assume she wasn't competitive or strong. But the truth was, Sarah never felt more alive than she did on the ball field. It didn't matter what the game was—soccer, baseball, basketball, even tennis. Having the chance to express herself via sports—it was just the greatest feeling in the world.

As soon as the playing field came into sight, Sarah spotted Jenna. She was standing off to the side talking to some boy, her dark hair blowing in the wind. Sarah ran over to her and tried to tap her on the back, but she was so excited, she practically tackled her accidentally. Jenna stepped forward to avoid falling over and laughed as she turned around. "Sarah, I presume?"

"Omigod! Sorry, Jenna."

"That's okay," Jenna replied, smiling. "I had a feeling you'd be pretty psyched this morning, since you didn't get sports last session. Sarah, this is David, a friend of my brother Adam. David, this is my friend Sarah." Jenna gestured to her friend. "She *really* likes sports."

David looked at Sarah and smiled. He was a little taller than Jenna, with messy, floppy brown hair and light green eyes. "Hey, Sarah," he said, holding out his hand. "Nice to meet you. I *really* like sports, too."

Sarah took David's hand to shake it, but he pulled it in, cinched it in his own, let it go, made a fist, bopped the top of her hand, then opened his hand and wiggled his fingers around her wrist. "Secret handshake," he told her in a low tone. "Keep it quiet. I only teach it to people I really like."

Sarah opened her mouth to say something—who *was* this guy?—but Jenna cut her off. "Hey, isn't that your friend from home?" she asked, gesturing over to the sidelines. "Andrea or Alli or something like that?"

Sarah followed her gaze to Abby's familiar face: wavy brown hair, brown eyes, freckles. For once, Sarah noted with some satisfaction, Abby looked a little unsure of herself. Without Gaby around, she didn't seem to know who to reach out to. Abby looked up and down the field, probably trying to find someone she recognized. When she didn't seem to find anyone, she frowned and started playing awkwardly with her hair. Sarah felt a little bad for her.

"Abby!" she yelled. Now that she was surrounded by friends and Abby had nobody, she figured she could afford to be nice.

Abby looked a little surprised to see Sarah calling for her, but her expression quickly turned to relief as she jogged over to the three of them. "Hey," she said. "Sarah, I would have walked over here with you, but by the time

I went looking for you, you were gone."

"Right," Sarah said. "Listen, this is my friend Jenna, we were in 3C together last year, and this is . . . David. Her brother's friend."

"Hi." Abby smiled and nodded awkwardly. "So, hey, I'm really psyched to get started. What do you think we're going to play today?"

Before any of them could answer, one of the counselors started yelling. "All right, everyone! Gather around here! I'm Keith, and I'm going to be your head coach for this session." Different members of the sports staff took turns running the electives each session.

All of the campers in sports—about twenty in all—started moving toward the center of the field, where Keith and three other counselors stood. When they formed a half circle around him, Keith continued. "This is Kimberly. She's going to be my assistant coach for this session. We're going to be trying something new for the next two weeks, so I hope you guys are feeling adventurous."

Sarah glanced over at Jenna. *Adventurous? What does he mean by that?*

"Donkey basketball," she heard David stage-whisper. *"Awesome."*

"Usually," Keith continued, oblivious to David's comment, "we kind of mix it up for the sports session. One day we'll play soccer, the next dodgeball, et cetera, et cetera."

"Have you ever played donkey basketball?" Sarah heard David whisper to Jenna. "It's like basketball but on donkeys. I wonder where they're going to get the donkeys?"

"*This* session," Keith was saying, "we're going to try something a little different. Kimberly and I were brainstorming last week, and we started thinking, wouldn't it be great to get you guys organized into teams and have some kind of tournament for the whole two weeks?"

"I don't think he's talking about donkeys," Sarah heard Jenna whisper to David.

"So ladies and gentlemen—" Here Keith reached down into a canvas bag that he had next to him and pulled out a bat and a big rubber ball. "—I give you, *softball!*"

"*WOOOOO!*" Sarah couldn't hold back a *whoop* of excitement. Softball! She was *awesome* at softball! Sure, she didn't play on the school team, but she'd played plenty of times at camp last year. This was *perfect!*

"Today, we're going to do some drills," Keith was saying. "Running, pitching, batting, all that jazz. The two boys and two girls who perform best at these drills will be made team captains and get to choose their players. Tomorrow, you guys will go into your new teams, get one practice day, and then we'll start the tournament the day after that." He waved his bat in the air. "Who's psyched for the first annual Camp Lakeview Softball Tournament?"

"*WOOOOO!*" The whole crowd erupted into cheers and applause.

Jenna turned to Sarah with a huge grin. "Sars, it's *totally* us. You and I have *got* to be the team captains."

"Don't be too sure about that!" Jenna and Sarah turned around to see Abby wearing a challenging grin. "I've heard you're a great athlete, Jenna, but I bet I can beat you!"

Jenna glanced at Sarah, and Sarah struggled not to roll her eyes. "She's on the team at school," Sarah said simply. "But that doesn't mean she'll win. Maybe we're better."

Abby gave Sarah a condescending look. "Have you ever *played* softball, Sarah?" she asked. "It might be tough for you if you don't know the rules."

Sarah gritted her teeth. "I've played," she replied.

"Well, we'll see who wins."

Jenna shot Sarah a look that said, *Who* is *this girl?* Sarah just shook her head. Meanwhile, the campers were separating out into boys and girls, as directed by Kimberly. David took off, waving behind him, and Sarah, Jenna, and Abby walked together to the first girls' drill—batting.

"I'll be following you from drill to drill," Kimberly, a redhead with curly bobbed hair, was explaining. "I'll keep track of how you do, but the only performance that matters is the best two girls'—those girls will become the team captains. All set?"

The girls looked one another over and nodded.

"Who wants to go first?"

As everyone kind of looked around, waiting for someone to speak up, Sarah saw her chance. *"I will,"* she volunteered.

Kimberly caught her eye and smiled encouragingly. "All right, then. Come on up and put on the batting helmet and get ready."

Sarah walked up to home plate. She tried to push the whole rest of the scene out of her mind as she pulled off her Red Sox hat, threw it to the side, and put on the blue plastic helmet. *Concentrate*, she told herself. *Forget about Abby, forget everyone watching you. You know you can do this. You have everything it takes to become team captain.*

Sarah leaned over and picked up the bat.

"Ready?" Kimberly called from several yards away, where she was winding up her pitch.

"Ready," Sarah replied. *Focus. Concentrate. Eye on the ball.*

She watched Kimberly lean back and wind up. It seemed to take an eternity for the ball to leave her hand, but finally it shot into the air, headed straight for her. Sarah tensed her shoulders and pulled back the bat. It felt perfect; she knew she had this pitch. She grinned and prepared herself for the sharp *crack* of the bat hitting the ball.

"*Goooooooo, Sarah!*" The words came from behind her, and it took a minute to place the voice. "*Come on! Winthrop Vikings in da house!*"

Abby. She's trying to break my concentration!

Sarah lost her concentration for only a second, but that was all it took. She was too late getting the bat over the plate; the ball sailed over without making contact. Sarah held onto the bat and turned to watch the ball sail by, in shock.

"*Strike one!*" Kimberly called.

▲   ▲   ▲

The next few drills went by in kind of a blur. Pitches flew past Sarah's bat, and it seemed like she needed some kind of divine intervention just to get a pitch over home plate. It was the worst athletic performance Sarah had ever seen, much less given herself. And the worst part was, she didn't know why it was happening.

That first strike, Sarah knew, could more or less be blamed on Abby. Abby's cheer broke her concentration, and she missed the ball. Simple enough. But after that, it was like Sarah was just *off*. Abby never said another word—in fact, she barely even looked in Sarah's direction, except for a smug little grin immediately after Sarah had struck out. But it was like Sarah could *feel* her watching everything she did. All she could think about, as the ball came toward her or she wound up to pitch, was how important it was to impress Abby.

Even Jenna noticed how off her game Sarah was—she started psyching Sarah up for every drill. "You can do it! This is your drill! Come on, Sars!"

But so far, it didn't seem to be working. It was like Sarah was a different person altogether: the bookish, quiet girl that Abby knew from back home. It was like Abby had been trying to morph her from Camp Sarah back into Home Sarah with that stupid cheer . . . and it had worked.

"All right," Kimberly was explaining as the girls arranged themselves for the catching drill. "I'm going to bat a few fly balls at you, and you try to catch them. Simple enough, right?"

Simple enough, Sarah thought. *Simple enough for me on any other day. But today it seems like all I know how to do is mess up.*

"Abby, how do you feel about starting us out?"

Sarah turned and watched as Abby walked up to the counselor, a big, expectant smile on her face. Of course, Abby had been performing like a champ all day. It was like she had been born with a bat in one hand and a glove on the other. It was kind of disgusting.

"Let's go, Abby!" Jenna yelled from Sarah's right. To add insult to injury, Jenna and Abby had spent the morning kicking butt. Sarah usually loved being around Jenna—she was so outgoing and fun—but she'd found herself wishing that the two girls would just wander off to the other side of the field and leave her alone. *Let me stink in peace,* she thought.

Sarah watched as Abby arranged herself on the field and effortlessly ran to catch a ball that sailed over her head and to the left. "Nice catch!" Kimberly shouted.

Jenna leaned over and poked Sarah's arm. "I can't believe you never told me what an incredible player Abby is," she whispered. "You must be on teams together!"

Sarah didn't respond. She'd never told Jenna that she didn't play on teams at home, or that she and Abby weren't friends.

Abby caught all five balls that were batted to her, and then it was time for the next girl.

"Who's up?" Kimberly asked.

Sarah looked around at the other girls. She knew that, given her performance on the other drills, she'd pretty much lost any shot she had at being one of the team captains. *But at least I can go out on a high note,* she thought. *I know how to catch. I've had an off day, but I can do this.*

"I'll go," she volunteered, and walked over to pick up the glove.

"GO, Sarah!" she heard Jenna yell. "You're awesome, Sarah! This is your comeback drill!"

Sarah tried to shut out all the noise around her

and concentrate on the ball. She held the glove out in front of her, ready to run in any direction. Kimberly tossed the ball into the air and easily sliced into it with the bat. Sarah watched as it sailed up . . . up . . . over her head and behind her, to the right. *I've got this. I've totally got this*, Sarah thought. She began jogging backward, her head tipped toward the sky, not wanting to lose track of the ball . . .

"*Aaaaaggghhh!*" Sarah's heel caught on something, and then she was flying backward, through space, until pain exploded in her head and everything went dark.

"Sarah?"

Sarah blinked and opened her eyes. It was like time had stopped; she was staring up into a blue sky. Around her, everything was quiet. Her right ankle was throbbing, and she didn't know why.

"Sars?" Suddenly Jenna's face eclipsed the sky, her brows furrowed, her mouth pulled into a concerned pout. Sarah stared up at her, wondering why she looked so worried.

"Yeah?" she asked.

"Sarah!" Suddenly, Kimberly's red head entered the frame. "That was quite a spill you took! It looks like you tripped over this tree root!"

"I—*ohhhhh*," Sarah murmured. Suddenly it all came back to her. The drills. The ball. She'd been running backward . . .

"Are you okay? I think you got the wind knocked out of you. Do you feel all right? Try to stand up."

Sarah pushed herself up on her elbows and looked around. She realized that not only Kimberly and Jenna were standing over her, but the whole girls' sports team was gathered around, and a few boys were scattered throughout the crowd.

"You okay?" a dark-haired, green-eyed boy was asking her, sort of urgently. What was his name again? *Oh yeah. David.*

"I'm a little dizzy," Sarah said honestly. "And my right ankle hurts."

"You'd better head over to the infirmary," Kimberly said. "Get it checked out, to be on the safe side. I can walk you over."

"No, that's okay." Jenna stepped forward and held a hand out to Sarah. "I'm her friend. If it's okay, I can take her."

Kimberly looked skeptical. "You'll need to support her to keep her weight off that ankle. I should probably still . . ."

"I can go, too!" Sarah found herself looking at whatshisname again. David. "We'll take full responsibility for her," he went on. "Jenna and I can walk her to the infirmary. We can wait until she's fixed up. We can even put a cast on her and sign it, if we need to."

Kimberly looked doubtful. She turned to Sarah. "Is that all right with you?"

Sarah shrugged. "Sure." It was a little weird that David wanted to go with them, but whatever. From what she'd seen so far today, *David* was a little weird. Maybe he'd just lost all interest in the drills when he realized that they weren't playing donkey basketball.

She grabbed Jenna's hand and hoisted herself up to a standing position. "I'm sure I'll be fine with them. Thanks."

Kimberly nodded. "Be careful not to put too much pressure on that ankle."

Jenna and David got on either side of Sarah, and she wrapped her arms around each of their shoulders, leaning on them and hopping on her left foot. "Thanks, guys," she said. *This day could not get worse*, she was thinking. *It's bad enough to screw up. It's worse to screw up in front of Abby. It's even worse than that to screw up in front of Abby, and then break my ankle or something.*

"I'm just glad to have an excuse to leave," David said cheerfully. "Was that the most boring session of sports you've ever had? 'Here, catch five hundred balls.' 'Here, run between these bases a million times.' I thought I'd fall asleep."

"I'm glad to be leaving," Sarah admitted, "but not because I was bored. Because I was *awful*. I thought I had a real shot at team captain, but I've never played so badly in my *life*. And now, who knows how long I'm going to be injured?"

"Think positively," Jenna said. "I'm sure your ankle will be fine—you just tripped. And as for screwing up, who cares? I mean, you just choked, Sars. Who knows why? Everyone chokes sometimes."

Sarah sighed. She didn't even like the sound of that. *Choked.* "You didn't," she told Jenna.

"Not today," Jenna replied. "But I have, before—a bunch of times. Like this one time at a gymnastics competition? I was supposed to do this whole routine on the balance bar, but I slipped before I even started and banged my head on the bar on the way down. I broke a tooth in front of everybody! *That's* choking."

Sarah nodded. It *did* make her feel a little better to hear that her crazy athletic friend had messed up, too. "Sorry, Jenna. And thanks."

"I can top that," David said. "This one time, my soccer team made it to the state championship. And I was trying to get the ball away from the other team, like, *really* hard. So I finally see my opening, and I get so excited that I just go on and kick the ball—I didn't pay any attention to where I was aiming, I just wanted to get it away from that guy. And would you believe, it flew right into the net—for *their* team? I scored a goal for the opposing team in the state championship. Yeah, my teammates were really psyched about that."

Sarah couldn't help laughing. "That's awful."

David nodded. "Because I messed up, we lost the championship."

Sarah glanced over at David. He still looked a little bummed about it, but he'd survived. He seemed like a cheerful guy. If he could mess up at the state championship, maybe it wasn't such a big deal to mess up at some camp drills.

Suddenly, Sarah became aware of David watching. "Are you *smiling*?" he asked. "Laughing at my pain? That's so not cool." But he was smiling, too.

Sarah shook her head and laughed awkwardly. "I am," she admitted. "I guess these stories do kind of make me feel better."

"Really? Well, I can top *that*," Jenna suddenly

piped up with a little smile. "This one time? My basketball team made it to the *national* championship."

"You never told me that!" Sarah broke in, but Jenna ignored her.

"And there was this girl on the other team who totally looked like a girl on *our* team. And I had the ball, and I got surrounded and had to pass, so then I see the girl from the other team—the one who *totally* looks like the girl on our team—and I passed the ball to her."

"Wow!" said Sarah.

"And we lost." Jenna nodded sadly.

"Wow," Sarah murmured. "I never knew that you had been to—"

"I can top *that*," David cut in.

"How can you top that?" Jenna demanded. She looked a little annoyed. In fact, Jenna and David were concentrating so hard on topping each other, they'd stopped moving. Fortunately, they were only a few yards from the infirmary. "We're talking *nationals*."

"This one time?" David began. "I was playing in a really important baseball game. It was a really important game, see, because my team hadn't won in a really long time. It was the championship, and we hadn't even been to the championships in, like, sixty-eight years."

Sarah glanced sideways at David. "Sixty-eight years, huh?"

David nodded. "That's right. The stands were packed. And I'm playing first base, and the ball comes to me, and I totally thought I had it. And the crowd is going nuts! So I reach for it, but it *rolls between my legs*."

"Between your *legs*?" Sarah asked. David started to

laugh. "Are you kidding me? David, that didn't happen to you!" Sarah cried. "That was Bill Buckner! The 1986 World Series! You're talking to a *huge* Red Sox fan."

David just cracked up in response, pulling away from Sarah. "You're right," he agreed, laughing. "I went too far. I got greedy."

"Does that mean—" Sarah turned around to face Jenna, who had also pulled away, and realized she was laughing, too. "Your basketball team never went to nationals! Why are you guys making stuff up?"

Jenna was laughing almost too hard to respond. Almost against her will, Sarah found herself smiling, too. Finally Jenna managed, "We were trying to cheer you up, Sars. It worked, right?"

Sarah looked from David to Jenna. They both looked very proud of themselves. "Well, right," she admitted.

"The point is, the drills today mean nothing," Jenna continued. "You'll play awesome once the tournament starts. That's what matters." She moved in next to Sarah and put Sarah's arm around her shoulders again. "And the gymnastics story was true, for the record. My front left tooth is bonded on. Now let's get you checked out."

David moved back in to support Sarah's other side. "See, there's a good example of someone choking and moving on," he said. "People eventually forgave Bill Buckner, right?"

Sarah looked at him like he was nuts. "You don't live in Boston, do you? No one forgave him until the Sox won the series in 2004! And you know what?

My dad still hasn't!"

△ △ △

"Sarah, you're going to be just fine." Helen, the camp nurse, was just finishing wrapping a thick Ace bandage around Sarah's ankle. "Just a minor sprain. You'll probably start feeling better later tonight."

"Oh, that's such a *relief!*" Sarah cried. She felt her whole body start to relax. "Does that mean I can stay in sports this session? That I'll be able to play?"

"Sure," Helen agreed with a smile. "I think today's session is over, but you'll be all healed and ready to play in a couple days. Now you and your friends can head over to lunch."

Sarah hobbled out to the waiting area with her bandaged foot. Jenna and David seemed to be locked in a heated game of rock, paper, scissors.

"Paper beats rock!" Jenna was saying.

"How does *paper* beat *rock?*" David argued with her. "I've got a *rock* here. It weighs, like, fifty pounds. You can cover my rock with paper, but so what? What does that get you?"

"*Ahem*," Sarah cut in, showing off her bandaged foot. "This is a really fascinating argument. But I'm ready. We can head to lunch now."

Jenna stood up and came running over to Sarah's side. "How does it feel? Is it broken?"

"No," Sarah explained. "Just sprained. The nurse says it's no big deal. It'll feel better within the next couple days, and I can start playing sports again."

"*Awesome*," David said, opening the door for Jenna

and Sarah. "Donkey basketball, here we come."

"There *is* no donkey basketball," Jenna snapped, annoyed.

"Is too."

"Is not."

"Sarah, can you say for sure that there's no donkey basketball? Keep in mind that the session is young. And there's a donkey farm right down the road."

Sarah's mind had already started to wander back to softball. "What was the question?"

She walked a little ahead of her friends, testing her weight on her sprained ankle. Nurse Helen had been right—it felt better already, wrapped up in the rigid bandage.

"There is *not* a donkey farm down the road," Jenna was saying. "That was a fair with a pony ride. And besides . . ."

Sarah let David and Jenna's voices fade into the background as she walked ahead. *So this wasn't such a bad day,* she told herself. *Sure, I was a lousy athlete, but we all have our off days. My ankle will be okay, and I have the next two weeks to prove myself. And I guess I kind of made a new friend.*

She glanced back at David, still bickering with Jenna. She wasn't sure yet whether that last part was a good or bad thing.

"*SARAH!*" Alex's voice was the first thing Sarah heard upon entering the mess hall. Lunch was already in session, and everyone was sitting with their bunkmates, eating hot dogs and beans.

Sarah hobbled over to 4C's table as Jenna and David splintered off to join their bunks.

"Thank goodness, you're okay!" Alex cried as Sarah sunk into her seat. "Abby told us you took this *huge* fall."

"It sounded really humiliating," Gaby added. Sarah noticed she was smiling a little.

"Yeah, I fell," Sarah replied simply. "It was no big deal. There was this tree root I didn't see."

"But it was a pretty crazy fall," Abby put in. "You were all like—*ahhhhh!*" Abby pantomimed falling backward off her seat. She wore a totally exaggerated, dopey expression, and spun her arms around in a wind-mill motion. Everyone at the table except Alex, Brynn, and Valerie laughed.

Sarah glared at her. "It wasn't *quite* like that," she said. "It happened really fast. Anyway, it really *hurt*, and I sprained my ankle."

"Awww!"

"Oh no!"

"You're going to be okay, right?"

Sarah heard her friends' expressions of concern, but she was still glaring at Abby, who was pretending not to notice. Abby wore a little smile as she picked at her baked beans. Sarah felt herself seething again. *It's all right that she doesn't want to be friends, but does she have to take pleasure in my pain?*

"Sarah?"

Sarah turned and looked into Grace's concerned face. *Oh. Right.* "I'll be fine," she replied, taking a sip of bug juice. "It's a minor sprain. It should heal up in a couple days, so I'll be able to play in the softball tournament, no problem."

"Good." Grace smiled. "I know how important sports are to you."

"Yeah." Candace grinned at Sarah. "To Sars, sports are, like, more important than *breathing!*"

Sarah could have sworn she heard Abby laugh. But when she turned around, Abby had covered it up with a loud cough.

"Anyway," Abby went on, "at least you weren't in contention for the captain spots. It would have stunk to have been playing really well, then have to go to the infirmary."

"I guess," Sarah muttered. "Anyway, who got to be captain?"

"Me!" Abby beamed. Sarah figured it was the biggest smile Abby had ever shown her—maybe the only smile. "I have a team, and this guy Kurt has another team. And guess what? I picked you for my team!"

Sarah was almost too stunned to answer. "You— what?"

Abby was still smiling. "I picked you for my team. I mean, everyone tells me you're this crazy incredible athlete, even if you were off your game today. I just figured, when you really take off, I want you on my team. I want to see it."

Sarah stared at Abby in confusion. *Is she being sincere?* Abby looked serious, but it was so hard to tell when you didn't know a person well.

"Great," she managed to croak in reply.

"That David kid is on our team, too. Actually, I put you both in the outfield, since you're friends."

He's not my friend, Sarah thought, and then

immediately felt bad. David was a little quirky, but he seemed nice enough. And she had the feeling it would be good to have a friendly face on the team.

"Great," Sarah replied.

"Great." Abby looked up from her meal and smiled.

This is going to be interesting, Sarah thought.

chapter
FOUR

All of Sarah's friends in 4C were super-sympathetic about her ankle. "Don't walk on it too fast," Alex warned her. "And don't feel bad for having to sit things out. You've got to give it time to get better."

At the campfire that night, Sarah already felt a lot better than she had that morning. Just being around her friends gave her a little charge, a little bit of confidence that being with Abby seemed to take away. Everyone seemed to think she'd be a huge asset to her team, even from left field. "Sars, you just have the *gift*," Brynn told her in a typically dramatic way. "Don't get all bent out of shape because you weren't great today. You'll be great again tomorrow."

Sarah, Alex, Grace, Candace, and Valerie were all leaning against the same log, sometimes taking part in the songs and storytelling, sometimes just whispering to each other. These lazy nights by the fire were one of Sarah's favorite things about camp: She always felt so safe and so happy, relaxing in the fire's orange glow with her friends. Already, her ankle was starting to feel better, and Sarah felt like her panic this morning was fading into the background. She believed Brynn's comforting words: She *was* great. And tomorrow, she'd get back to showing Abby just how great.

"Who's that kid I saw you walking with earlier?" Alex asked. "Some boy, with messy brown hair?"

"Oh, that was David." Sarah smiled a little rueful smile. "He's a friend of Adam's, I guess. He's a little weird."

"Good weird or bad weird?" Brynn asked with a smile.

"Since when are there two kinds of weird?" Sarah asked. "Just *weird,* weird. He kept talking about donkey basketball and then pretended he was Bill Buckner."

"Who's Bill Buckner?" Val asked.

"Never mind."

Alex smiled. "I thought he might be some guy you had a crush on. Maybe someone you'd want to go to the dance with."

Sarah stared at her friend in disbelief. "*What?* No."

Alex shrugged and turned around to face the fire. "I was thinking I might ask Geoff Darden, from 5G? I think he's kind of cute." She sunk down into her sweatshirt and blushed.

Sarah felt stab of annoyance. Around her, all her other friends were *oohing* like this was some big secret.

"You know *I* think he's cute, Al," Brynn spoke up. "Even though he's a little older. Kind of reminds me of Orlando Bloom. Like in the eyes?"

"Are you *crazy?*" Sarah asked. "He's fourteen. He doesn't look anything like Orlando Bloom."

"*I* think he does," Alex agreed. "Brynn, what's going

on with your crush?"

Sarah looked from Alex to Brynn and back again. She felt like she was in the wrong bunk. Alex barely *knew* this Geoff kid. Why was she so excited?

Brynn sighed. "I don't know. Nothing really, yet. But I would like to ask someone to the dance with me. I definitely want to have a date this year."

"What?" cried Sarah, but her voice was covered by Candace's, who spoke up at the same time.

"I want to have a date this year, too," she was saying.

"You know what we should do?" Brynn piped up suddenly, looking all excited. "I just had this great idea!"

"What?" Alex asked.

Brynn smiled. "We should make a pact. All of us will bring dates this year!"

Sarah's stomach dropped. She couldn't believe this was happening. Who *were* these people?

"That's a great idea!" said Grace. "If we all have to do it, it will give us some confidence. Like, I'll feel more comfortable asking a guy if I know all of you are doing the same thing."

"Right!" Valerie smiled. "Besides, it will be fun to all have dates. It's more fun to have someone to dance with."

"We *do* have someone to dance with," Sarah spoke up. Everyone kind of looked at her like she was nuts, but she plowed ahead. "Each other. Remember? We all dance in a big circle and have an awesome time. Since when are all of you guys so into boys?"

Sarah's friends all looked surprised by her outburst, and a little sheepish. Sarah didn't get why they were surprised—she'd never been boy crazy like this. But then again, they hadn't, either. Sarah felt like everyone else had gotten a card in the mail telling them to act totally different, and she was left wondering what happened. They were all looking at her like she was the weird one—but she was the only *normal* one. Right?

"I'm not *into* boys," Alex said defensively. "I don't know what you mean by that. I'm not obsessed or anything. I mean, Priya is friends with Jordan. Maybe we can be friends with boys, too."

Sarah just looked at her, doubtful.

"Me neither," Brynn agreed. "I wouldn't say I'm *into* boys. Just . . . kind of interested."

Sarah didn't know what to say, so she didn't say anything. She was starting to feel like maybe she was being unreasonable—maybe *they* were the normal ones. But she couldn't help the way she felt . . . like her friends were changing everything. For the worse.

"There's nothing wrong with being kind of interested," Alex said. "I mean, we're getting older now. Things change, Sars."

Sarah was glad for the dim firelight because she felt her cheeks burning. *How does that make it okay? What about great things that change into awful things?* Again, she didn't say anything, just stared into the fire. After a few minutes, Val started telling a funny story about what she'd done in ceramics that morning, and the boy discussion was forgotten.

Still, when everyone was chuckling about Val's messed-up vase, Sarah snuck away and went to sit with Jenna.

Sarah wasn't sure what woke her up the next morning. Suddenly, she was awake in her bunk, but it was darker and quieter than when she normally woke up. And something was going on. She heard her friends rousing, their bunk beds creaking as they strained to see what was going on.

Then she heard it again: the same sound that must have woken her up.

"AAAAAAAUUUUGH!"

Gaby! It was Gaby's scream, and it was coming from the bathroom! Sarah struggled out of her sleeping bag and started running for the bathroom, trying to make sense of all this in her head. Gaby was always up bright and early, making sure that she'd have plenty of time in the bathroom.

When Sarah reached the bathroom, most of her bunkmates were gathered around Gaby, who was clutching a towel around herself just outside the first shower stall. Gaby looked bleary-eyed and confused, with a weird pinkish streak running over her left shoulder. Sarah could hear the water still running. She glanced inside and saw that the water coming from the showerhead was bright *red*!

"It's blood," Gaby whimpered, still half-asleep.

Fortunately, Becky was standing right next to Gaby, and she reached her hand up to the showerhead to cup some red water in her hand. "It's not blood," she said gently, sniffing. "It's just red."

"How do you know?" Gaby asked as Becky

examined the liquid.

"Well, blood doesn't smell like strawberries, for one thing." The girls gathered closer as Becky leaned down and sniffed the liquid again, then gingerly touched her tongue to it. *Aha.* Girls, I think we have an answer."

"What is it?" Alex cried at the same time as Abby and Val.

"Bug juice!" Becky replied with a big smile. "And I bet I can tell how it got in there. Girls, if someone can just get me the tool kit . . ."

Sarah ran to the tiny bathroom closet and pulled out a small tool kit in a black plastic case, emblazoned with 4C. She ran over to Becky and handed it to her. "Here you go."

Becky quickly opened the kit and fished out a pair of pliers. Then she turned off the shower, stepped inside, and began twisting off the showerhead. After a lot of twisting with the pliers, and then with her hands, the showerhead finally plopped off into Becky's hand. She glanced into the back, then smiled and held the shower-head out to the campers.

"Oooooh," they all murmured, taking in the soaked red powder that coated the inside of the showerhead.

"Bug-juice mix," Becky announced. "Girls, I think we've been pranked."

"But how is that possible?" Gaby cried. "When could they have gotten in here? While we slept?"

"Either that or last night," Sarah replied. "They could've come during the campfire. No one showered till this morning."

Becky nodded, then walked over to the next shower and turned on the water. Sure enough, it also came out bright red—bug juice red. "We'd better clean out these showerheads," Becky said. "Then we can all take our showers." She started removing the second showerhead.

"Who would do this?" Candace asked. "I mean, we're not really at war with anybody. Are we?"

Alex shrugged. "Aren't we kind of *always* at war with 4A?" she asked. "Besides, this has Jenna written all over it."

Sarah wasn't so sure. If this had been done during the campfire last night—well, she'd been sitting with Jenna and the rest of 4A for half of it. But then, it might have been done in the middle of the night. And Jenna was the master prankster . . . she could definitely see Jenna sneaking into their cabin in the middle of the night like a spy.

"If that's true," Valerie said, "don't we owe them a prank back? A *good* one. We're not going to let Jenna and 4A ruin our morning showers and not get them back!"

"We are sooooo getting them back for this!" Gaby cried, gathering up her soap and shampoo. "I hope they're happy now. Taking their normal-colored showers. Because we're going to come up with the prank to end all pranks!"

"Huh?" Jenna scrunched up her eyebrows and crossed her arms in front of her chest. "Bug juice in the showerheads? Why didn't I think of that?"

"Are you saying you *didn't* think of it?" demanded Alex, poking her finger in Jenna's face in full-interrogation mode. "Are you saying it was the work of someone else? And if so, who?"

"Who?" Jenna uncrossed her arms and looked at Alex as if she was nuts. "How should I know, Alex?"

"Who else would have the *motive*, Jenna?" Brynn asked in a typically overdramatic way, flailing her arms around like the craziest lawyer ever. "Why would any other bunk want to mess with 4C? You want to mess with us because you know we're awesome, and you're *jealous*." Brynn broke into a huge grin as the rest of 4C looked on.

Jenna looked from Brynn to the rest of her bunk—a long row of curious, annoyed faces. Sarah had thought she would laugh, or at least smile, but she didn't. Actually, she looked kind of upset. "Look, I don't know what you're talking about," she said. She started walking toward the mess hall.

Brynn watched her go, putting her hand to her face and stroking her chin. "I didn't hear an alibi," she murmured.

"I don't think she did it," Sarah admitted. "Remember, she swore she was going to be good this year."

Gaby looked thoughtful. "I don't believe that for a minute," she said. "This is *Jenna* we're talking about. She talks a good game, but isn't that part of the whole Jenna *thing*? She wants to be the best prankster at camp, and to be a good prankster, you've gotta be able to lie."

"Are you saying she's just getting better at denying it?" Candace asked. There was a nervous little crease between her eyebrows, like she was too tired to follow this conversation.

"That's *exactly* what I'm saying," said Gaby. "But two can play at that game, right? Or ten."

"So—we need to think of a prank for 4A?" Sarah asked. "Is that what you're saying?"

"That's what I'm saying," Gaby agreed. "And it better be good."

Sarah's ankle still felt a little touchy that morning, so she spent sports sitting on the sidelines, trying to get a feel for her team. There was no doubt about it: Abby was amazing. She was a great pitcher, with a lightning-fast fastball, but she was a good batter, too, earning two singles and a home run in the first game. Sarah sighed, pulling some blades of grass from the ground and balling them up into little rubbery clumps. She definitely had her work cut out for her if she was going to impress Abby.

Later, in arts and crafts, Sarah tried to copy Alyssa as they used dusty chalk pastels to draw a peaceful forest scene. "I'm awful at this," Sarah complained. "It's like some drawing chip my brain is missing."

Alyssa leaned over and smudged the corner of Sarah's picture with her thumb. Some of the bright yellow chalk blurred and blended into a reasonable copy of the sunny sky. "See? It's not so bad," Alyssa said. "You just have to know how to work with the materials."

Sarah smiled. It was somehow relaxing being

around Alyssa, especially after the weird, bug-juice morning and stressing herself out over sports. "Gaby is going nuts about the prank you guys pulled on us this morning," she confided. "If I were in 4A, I'd be getting prepared for some serious revenge."

Alyssa just rolled her eyes and sketched in a pine tree with a heavy, dark-green line. "Oh, right, the infamous prank that Jenna supposedly did?" She shrugged. "I don't know anything about it."

"But isn't that what you would say even if you *did* know something about it?" Sarah asked suspiciously.

Alyssa just shrugged and laughed. "I guess."

"Well." Sarah sketched in a log covered with moss, then layered some lighter green over the dark colors to show the light hitting the moss. She smudged with her finger and was pretty impressed by the result. "Alyssa?" she asked.

"Yeah?"

Sarah busied herself getting the wildflowers on the forest floor just right, not wanting to look Alyssa in the eye. "Are you bringing a date to the social?"

Alyssa looked surprised, then considered for a few seconds, working on her drawing. "A date?" she asked. "I don't think so. I mean, I'm sure Natalie will go with Simon."

"Sure, sure." Natalie had been dating Simon since the summer before. Sarah wondered if she had just made herself look like a little kid, making too big of a deal out of the whole date thing.

"I don't know who *I* would go with," Alyssa went on. "I mean, unless some artsy, journal-y kind of guy with dreamy blue eyes comes up to me from out of nowhere, you know?"

Sarah smiled. "Blue eyes, huh?"

Alyssa nodded. "That's my thing. But Adam and I aren't really hanging out this year, and I haven't met anyone else who floats my boat, so I'll probably be going to the social stag." She glanced sideways at Sarah. "Are *you* bringing a date?"

Sarah shook her head. "I'm not really into dating," she said. "But it's like everyone in 4C took a dating pill last week. They're all talking about who they're going to bring, how many slow songs they want them to play. They all volunteered for the social committee."

Alyssa nodded. "Yeah. Natalie, Chelsea, and Tori are all doing that, too."

Sarah sighed. "I just . . . I dunno." She added a fuzzy tail to a squirrel she'd sketched in. "I feel like everything's changed so much this year. First we all got split up, then everyone went nuts for the social, then—" Sarah stopped herself just before she said "Abby showed up at camp." None of her friends were close with Abby, but they all seemed to think she was cool. Sarah didn't want to look mean by looking like the only one who didn't like her.

Alyssa glanced up at her sympathetically, then turned back to her sketch. "That's true," she said. "But everything changes. Some things get worse, but some things get better, right?" She looked up and smiled.

Sarah looked at her for a moment before smiling back. *I guess,* was what she wanted to say. *I sure liked it better before, though.* But even to her ears that sounded whiny and childish. Finally she let her lips turn up. "Right," she said. "You're so wise, Alyssa."

Alyssa just laughed. "I'll send you a bill with my fee."

▲ ▲ ▲

When Sarah got back to the cabin before dinner, her bunk was already buzzing about something. Sarah had passed Becky outside, talking on her cell phone, and Sophie was sacked out on her bunk, taking a nap. All of her bunkmates were huddled together on three bottom bunks, whispering.

"We have to do it *tonight*," Gaby was saying, "for maximum impact." She looked up when Sarah walked into the room. "*Sars!*" she hissed. "I'm so glad you're back. You'll *love* my idea for getting revenge on 4A! It's a much better prank than bug juice in the showers!"

Sarah nodded skeptically and settled lightly on the edge of a bunk. "Okay," she agreed. "Um . . . what is it?"

Gaby exchanged glances with Grace and Brynn, who nodded eagerly. "All right. It's kind of similar to what they did to us, in that we sneak into their cabin in the middle of the night and do something to the bathroom. But *this* . . ." She had to pause as she descended into a fit of giggles. "This is *so* much better! Honestly, I should be planning pranks all the time."

Sarah just nodded. She wasn't totally convinced that Gaby was on Jenna's level. She knew Gaby would like to think she was, but in Sarah's opinion, she didn't quite have the *fun* that you needed to have—she didn't have the prankster's sensibility. Gaby could be funny, but she could also be mean-spirited, and in Sarah's experience, mean-spirited pranks only led to trouble.

"Here it is." Gaby instinctively lowered her voice, and all the campers leaned in close to hear her. "We wait until Becky and Sophie are asleep tonight. Then, three of us sneak out and in the back door of 4A's cabin. We go into the bathroom and—and—"

Here Gaby collapsed into a fit of giggles. Some of the other girls—Brynn, Alex, and Candace—started laughing, too. Sarah snuck a glance at Abby. She was sitting with her face arranged in an *almost* smile, like she wasn't sure what to make of any of this.

"—we *steal* all of their toilet paper!"

Gaby started laughing uncontrollably and put her head down to recover. Most of the campers gathered around started laughing, too, even Abby, though she still looked a little confused.

"We steal all of their toilet paper!" Candace echoed, delighted. "It's perfect!"

Sarah let out a few awkward giggles. "Um . . ." she began, "isn't that kind of *mean*? I mean, no toilet paper is more of an . . ."—she tried to think of an appropriate word—". . . *inconvenience* than having bug juice in the shower, you know? Not being able to go to the bathroom versus getting a little sticky in the shower . . . I think it's worse."

Gaby started a fresh round of giggles. "I know!" she cried. "That's why it's the perfect comeback prank!"

"But doesn't that raise the stakes?" asked Valerie, who, Sarah now noticed, also looked less than convinced. "I mean, we steal their toilet paper . . . who knows what they'll do to *us*?"

Gaby recovered from her giggles for long enough to put on a serious face. "Val," she said, "pranking is a tough business. They call it a prank *war* for a reason. I have nothing to offer you but blood, sweat, and . . . maybe no toilet paper the day after tomorrow. But that's what pranking's about. If you don't have the stomach for it, then . . ." She shook her head doubtfully.

Val nodded. "Well, I don't have the stomach for it," she said. "But it doesn't matter, because when they retaliate, they're doing it to all of us. Anyway"—she glanced at Sarah—"they already decided who's going tonight. And too bad for us, we're out of it."

Sarah nodded. She had to admit, she felt relieved. "Who's going then?"

"Me, Alex, and Grace," Gaby said. "We figured it out at the social-committee meeting."

Sarah felt her stomach sink. She hadn't even wanted to go, but hearing that they'd figured this whole thing out without asking her hurt a little bit. She was beginning to wonder whether she'd made a mistake not signing up for the social committee. She really didn't care about the social at all, but she felt like she was missing out on valuable time with her friends.

"All right, then," Sarah said quietly, hoping that someone would pick up on the hurt in her voice. "I guess it's all decided."

"Right," agreed Gaby, totally oblivious. Suddenly she looked up, toward the doorway. "Shhh," she whispered. "Ixnay on the ankpray alktay."

Becky burst into the room with a big smile. "You guys ready for dinner?" she asked. "We should start

walking over. Someone go in there and wake up Sophie."
She turned and started heading out of the cabin. "I don't
know about you guys, but I have the worst craving for bug
juice!"

"Not funny, Becky," Gaby muttered as she and the
rest of the campers all rose to their feet. "*So* not funny."

"*Psssst.*"

It was just a tiny noise. Like a mouse noise, maybe,
or an ant farting. Sarah tried to ignore it. It was the middle
of the night, and she was in the middle of a very cool
dream about joining the Red Sox and somehow, at the
same time, curing cancer. It was one of those amazing
coincidences that only happen in really good dreams. She
turned away from the mouse noise and snuggled deeper
into her pillow.

"Psssst. *Sarah.*"

Now the ant was farting her name. This was
serious. She opened her eyes just a crack and looked at
her pillow. It was just as she'd left it: down-filled with a
Red Sox pillowcase. No mice or ants. Sarah was trying
to build up the energy to turn over when Grace's voice
suddenly became clear.

"*Sarah.* Wake *up*, sister!" A hand reached out and
shoved her shoulder.

"*What?*" Sarah hissed as she turned over. Now
that she was fully awake, she realized how much more
fun she'd been having asleep. *What are the chances of
falling into a joining the Red Sox/curing cancer dream again? That
combination doesn't happen every day.*

"Sars, you have to get up and help us with the prank."

"Ankpray!" came Gaby's forceful whisper from the darkness. "Keep it down, Grace!"

"Right, the ankpray," Grace continued, softening her voice. "*Anyway*. Alex won't wake up, so we need an extra person."

Sarah looked at Grace and rubbed her eyes. "So you chose me?" She didn't know whether to feel touched or not.

"Of course!" Grace smiled. "Well, we tried Val, too. But she must have been having a really good dream or something. She threw her teddy bear at me and knocked me off her bunk."

Always one step ahead of me, that Val. Sarah took a deep breath and raised herself up out of her sleeping bag. She looked down and saw Gaby standing by the door of the cabin, clutching her empty duffel bag. "All right," Sarah whispered. "But you both owe me."

"Sure," her friends whispered in unison as she swung her legs out of the sleeping bag and onto the floor. Her ankle had finally stopped hurting, she noted with satisfaction. Stepping carefully in the dark, Sarah raised herself up and slipped on her flip-flops. She grabbed her hooded sweatshirt from the cubby, ran a quick hand through her hair, and walked toward the door.

"Let's go."

Gaby and Grace followed as Sarah began leading the way toward 4A's cabin down the trail. The air was chilly and felt cool in her lungs. Actually, it was kind of fun being out at this time of night—even if she wasn't totally convinced that the prank was a good idea. Sarah tried to make it sound better in her mind as she walked silently through the dark. *It's all in good fun. Besides, if Jenna really was behind the prank this morning—and she probably was—they deserve to be hit back. And sure, it's a little crude, but it's a great revenge prank, right? Right!* Sarah tried to quiet the contrary voices in her mind—like the one that said Jenna didn't seem to be behind the prank this morning, or the one that said messing with toilet paper was a level of nastiness she didn't want to sink to. Sarah looked around at the faces of Gaby and Grace, her good buds. She was out in the cool night air with her friends, having some fun, and that was all that mattered.

"All right," Gaby whispered as they approached the cabin. "We have to be *super*-quiet. Quieter than quiet! If anyone hears us, we're sunk."

Grace and Sarah nodded obediently.

"We'll sneak in the back door, right to the bathroom. Sarah, you take the right stall; I'll take the middle; Grace, you take the left. We'll remove the TP and put it in this duffel bag. Before we leave, we'll check the supply closet and take out any extra. That make sense?"

Grace and Sarah nodded again. "Aye aye, captain," Grace whispered.

"Good. Are you ready?"

"Yup."

"Yup."

Gaby nodded solemnly. "Okay. Ladies, let's move in."

They snuck over to the back door, a crude

wooden door with a latch and no screen. Gaby silently lifted the latch, then pulled back the door and gestured to Grace and Sarah to go in. The door creaked a tiny bit on its hinges, but nobody stirred. In the bathroom, the girls all tiptoed to their assigned stalls. Sarah carefully pulled out the toilet paper roll, walked out of the stall, and placed it silently in Gaby's bag. When all three were done, Gaby headed to the supply closet beside the showers and opened it up. There were six extra rolls of toilet paper on the second shelf, and Gaby carefully grabbed them one by one and placed them into the bag. Then she looked at Grace and Sarah and nodded. She pointed wordlessly to the back door.

When they slipped out of the back door without incident, Sarah had to admit to herself that they'd pulled it off beautifully. She was even a little surprised. Part of her had been convinced that someone in 4A would wake up to use the bathroom in the middle of the raid and find the three of them with their arms full of toilet paper. But when they got back to 4C and high-fived one another, Sarah was pretty sure they'd gotten away with it.

"Awesome!" whispered Gaby. "Good job, ladies."

"What do we do with the toilet paper?" Sarah asked. It suddenly occurred to her that a duffel bag full of toilet paper rolls might look a little suspicious to Becky.

"I already thought of that," whispered Gaby. "We'll just put them in our supply closet, shoved in the back. Nobody will notice."

Sarah nodded. "Cool."

Grace beamed at both of them. "Guys, this was so much fun! I really think we got them back good. That will teach them to mess with us!"

"Yeah," Gaby agreed, looking starry-eyed. "This might just be the prank to end all pranks!"

Sarah nodded very slowly. "Yeeeah," she agreed. "Well, um, I'm going back to bed."

▲ ▲ ▲

"You *rats.*"

Sarah blinked as she finished tying the laces on her sneakers. She was exhausted this morning, because she'd been too excited to fall back asleep after the prank. Natalie and Chelsea were standing in the cabin doorway. And they looked pretty mad.

"Worse than rats," Natalie corrected Chelsea. "Rats just steal other people's garbage because they're hungry. They don't go around stealing *basic human necessities*—like toilet paper!"

The two girls stormed through the cabin toward the bathroom. Natalie was from New York. *She knows the finer points of rat behavior,* thought Sarah. She, Abby, Gaby, and Valerie—her bunkmates who were awake and ready in the bedroom—followed the blaze of indignation into the bathroom. There, Natalie had already opened up the supply closet, and was loading toilet paper into Chelsea's waiting arms.

"How *convenient,*" Natalie was saying. "They just happen to have—let's see—*nine* extra rolls of toilet paper. How interesting, considering that in all of 4A, we have *none.*"

Chelsea nodded thoughtfully. "It does raise some questions," she agreed. "Like, who would be so immature as to steal toilet paper? And why on earth, since it's been established that we did *not* prank 4C the other night?"

"I think the immaturity question is the more interesting one," Natalie went on. "Considering that, even if they suspect Jenna of pranking them, that's no reason to punish *all* of 4A to make up for it."

"Especially those who wake up early to answer the call of Mother Nature!" Chelsea finished.

"Yes," Natalie agreed, handing a final roll to Chelsea and narrowing her eyes at the assembled 4C campers. "*Especially* those people. But you know, Chelsea, it's all right—I'm sure these girls know about karma."

"Ooh, karma," Chelsea repeated, backing out of the bathroom and turning to head out of the cabin. "What goes around comes around."

"That's right," said Natalie. "So we can only imagine what will come around as revenge for this. Ta-ta, ladies."

"Ciao," said Chelsea.

And then they were gone, ends of toilet paper flapping behind them.

Valerie looked at Gaby. "I *told* you. Now who knows what they're going to do to us."

Gaby just shrugged, looking satisfied. "We'll deal with that when it comes. For now . . ." She smiled. "We just savor the feeling of a job well done." She paused. "And keep an extra roll of toilet paper in your cubby, just in case."

chapter
SIX

"You all are *so* dead."

Jenna stood in front of 4C's table in the mess hall, looking furious. Her arms were folded, and her eyes shot daggers at Gaby. *Even her hair looks angry,* Sarah thought sleepily. She took another bite of pancakes as Gaby returned Jenna's glare.

"You know what they say about karma, Jenna," Gaby said airily, sipping her OJ. "What goes around comes around."

"Look." Jenna's voice was sharp and gravelly. "I am going to say this one more time, very slowly. I. Did. Not. Put. Bug Juice. In. Your. Showers. I did *not* put the *stupid* bug juice in your *stupid* showers. Okay? But now I kind of wish I did, because you totally had it coming and I didn't even realize it yet."

Gaby regarded Jenna coolly, slowly chewing her pancakes. "That doesn't even make sense."

"I *mean* you were . . ." Jenna sighed. "Forget it. Look, all that matters is you have got some serious payback coming. All of you." She slowly looked around the table, taking time to lock eyes with every camper. "I'd learn to sleep with one eye open, if I were you guys." With that, she turned on her heel and stalked back to her table.

Sarah took a sip of her juice and swallowed as everyone seemed to process Jenna's threat. "If she really did put the bug juice in our showers, she's a great actress," she said quietly.

"Oh, she did it," Gaby said with certainty. "She's just mad we figured it out. And sure, she'll get us back . . . but we'll get her back even harder."

Maybe it was lack of sleep, but this whole prank war was sounding stupider to Sarah than it had ever seemed before. *What will be missing when we wake up tomorrow?* she wondered. *The toilets? Our bunk beds? Will all of our underwear be floating in the lake?* Her concern was made greater by the nagging feeling that Jenna really *hadn't* pranked them first. *But if not her, who did it?* she wondered. She couldn't come up with any candidates at all. Really, they didn't *know* the other campers well enough for them to want to prank 4C.

It was a mystery. But one thing was for certain: All of 4C had better be on the lookout for Jenna's revenge.

▲ ▲ ▲

"Two, four, six, eight! Who do panthers love to hate? Tigers! *Tigers!* TIIIIGERRRS!"

Sarah's ankle was feeling back to normal, and she was *finally* getting the chance to play softball. Unfortunately, she was still stuck in left field—nowheresville—with the strangest boy at Camp Lakeview. David was playing center field and making up silly cheers to pass the time. The cheers seemed to annoy the heck out of Abby, who cast an evil glare in his direction from the pitchers mound every five seconds. David either didn't notice or did a great job of pretending not to notice. The whole thing would have made Sarah want to laugh . . . if she weren't incredibly depressed to be stuck in left field.

It was the third inning and not a single ball had come in Sarah's direction. David had caught the ball exactly once and immediately made up a cheer describing how great he was. Sarah felt miserable. She'd psyched herself up to impress Abby once they started playing. Now she wasn't sure what was worse: playing in a game and performing badly or not even having the chance to perform at all. It seemed entirely possible that she could spend the whole two weeks out in left field, watching grass grow and memorizing David's cheers, and never once see the ball come in her direction. *Why is my life like this?* Sarah wondered miserably. *Did Abby put me out here on purpose, so I'd never get the chance to prove myself? Why is life so unfair?*

"Tiii-gers! Tiii-gers! We like to play all day! Tiii-gers! Tiii-gers! We don't care what you say! WE ARE AWESOME! WE ARE AWESOME! WE ARE—"

"*DAVID!!!*" Abby paused mid-throw and turned around on the pitcher's mound to glare at him. "*STOP! CHEERING! NOW!* You're breaking my concentration!"

Sarah looked at David, expecting him to look crushed, or at least a little embarrassed. Instead, he shooed a fly away from his face, shrugged, and punched his glove. "Whatever you say, captain. I'm just trying to build up a little team spirit."

Abby rolled her eyes, grabbing the ball again and

returning to her post. "Well, do it *silently*."

David nodded. Abby turned back around and wound up for her pitch. David mouthed silent cheers while waving his hands around behind her. For the third time that day, Abby threw an awesome curveball and struck out the batter. "Strike one!" yelled Kimberly, the coach who was watching their game. "Nice job, Abby."

Nice job, Abby. Nice job, Abby. Yeah, so nice, you're not even letting them hit *the ball,* Sarah thought bitterly. *The rest of us might as well not even be here. It's like a one-woman show.*

"Psssst."

Sarah looked over and saw David gesturing to her. "You bored?" he asked, quietly enough for only her to hear.

She turned around and tried to ignore him. *I have to pay attention to the game,* she told herself. *A ball might come out here any minute. I have to be ready.* She punched her glove, trying to get it all hollowed out and ready for her face-saving catch. *Yup, any minute now. Any minute now the ball will come out here.*

The new batter fouled a couple times, then finally hit a fly ball to third base, which the third baseman, Casey, caught easily. *Darn,* thought Sarah. The next batter hit a single, fielded by the shortstop. *Double darn.* The next batter was a boy that Abby had struck out in the first inning. One strike. Two strikes. Sarah sighed loudly and rubbed her eyes. Three strikes . . . inning over.

"All right, Tigers!" Kimberly yelled enthusiastically. "Nice job! You're up at bat!"

Sarah shuffled out of left field, feeling heavy all over. *This is such a joke,* she thought. *How am I going to impress anyone out there?* She was an okay batter but had walked in the first inning, then hit a pop fly in the second. She felt that if she was going to do something impressive, it wouldn't be at bat.

"Aren't you *bored?*" David asked, taking off his glove and stretching his fingers. "I know I am. We hardly ever get the ball!"

"At least they batted to you once," Sarah muttered. "The ball hasn't come to me at all. I might as well not even be out there."

David nodded. "That's why I started with the cheers," he said. "I thought it would be fun, you know? Nothing serious." He glanced at Abby, who was instructing Casey on the finer points of swinging the bat. "But Abby is such a drill sergeant. I wish she'd just let us have fun."

Sarah watched Abby swinging the bat for Casey. She was talking loudly, stopping to point at her shoulders and the position of her elbows. *At least I'm not the only person who doesn't like her,* she thought. *She can be kind of bossy.*

"She goes to my school," Sarah told David quietly as they took their seats on the bench.

David nodded. "I remember Jenna said something like that," he said. "What's she like?"

Sarah shrugged. *Sporty. Outgoing. The opposite of me.* "A jock," she said simply.

David nodded slowly. "What are *you* like?" he asked.

Sarah looked at his face, which arranged in a surprisingly interested expression. He looked like he really cared what she had to say. "*Not* a jock," she replied, with a nervous laugh.

David smiled and nodded seriously. "I hear you," he said. "We can't all be Curt Schilling, you know?"

"I know," Sarah agreed. "Believe me."

Two more innings went by with nothing much happening. The Tigers were winning, 4-3, but not because of anything Sarah had done. She managed to make a single in the fourth inning, but the inning was over before she could get to second, and the ball stubbornly refused to come into the left field. She tried to pay attention, to care what was happening, but she was quickly losing her drive. *What does it matter what your team is doing if you don't have any part in it?* she wondered. Sarah was used to being the star of the team, an athlete that people paid attention to. It was an unsettling feeling, just blending into the crowd.

David was amusing himself quietly. When Abby wasn't looking, he tossed his glove into the air and caught it or drew tic-tac-toe games in the dirt. When he noticed Sarah looking at him, he would grin and try to do something funny. Stick his glove on his head and try to walk while balancing it there, like he was on *America's Next Top Model*. Or do a cartwheel. (He couldn't even come close, but he tried.) Sarah tried not to be distracted, but it was really hard. When he stuck his arms out and started dancing with an imaginary partner, tangoing some invisible lady around center field, complete with dips and kicks, Sarah couldn't help it anymore. She started laughing. And the more she laughed, the more David played it up. He started shaking his hips. Spinning his "partner" around. Pretending to throw her up in the air and catch her as she came down. Sarah started laughing so hard, she was having trouble breathing and had to snort through her nose. She doubled over, covering her mouth and trying to calm down. *It's not even that funny,* she thought. *Why is it when David does things they seem funnier than they really are?*

"SARAH!"

Sarah suddenly straightened up. That was Abby's voice. Abby was yelling at her—but why? Then Sarah saw it. *The ball. In left field. Omigod.*

It was headed toward the far left fence, as far from Sarah as it could possibly be. Sarah vaulted after it, putting out a superhuman effort to get to that side of the field. But it just wasn't possible, not now. Not after she'd quit paying attention to crack up at David's clowning around.

Everything seemed to move in slow motion as Sarah made one final leap toward the ball, but fell far short. The ball sailed soundlessly over the fence. Sarah let out a cry and fell flat out on the ground with a *whump*. The hard ground knocked the breath from her lungs and left her stunned and sore. She heard feet pounding on the dirt as the opposite team's players ran the bases.

"A *grand slam!* Nice job!" Kimberly shouted. "Four points! That puts you in the lead, Panthers—7-3!"

Sarah blinked. She had done it. She had lost the game for the Tigers. She'd just finished convincing herself that she had no effect on the game's outcome whatsoever. And just like that, everything changed, and suddenly she'd had a *huge* effect—for the worse.

I wonder if I just lie here forever and don't get up, if eventually they'd start playing around me. Sarah looked closely at the grass around her head. There was an ant crawling on a dandelion. A leaf curled around a stem. It all seemed like great stuff to look at—much better than looking at Abby's disappointed face. *I don't believe I just did that*, Sarah thought. *Now she'll hate me more than ever.*

"You okay?" At the sound of his voice, Sarah looked up into David's concerned face. He held out a hand, and Sarah grabbed it and pulled herself up to her knees, then to her feet. She felt Abby's gaze on her so strongly that it was like a magnet pulling her eyes to that direction. And there Abby was—her eyebrows furrowed, her lips pulled down into a frown. *She can't believe it*, Sarah thought. *She can't* believe *how bad I am.*

Abby shook her head. "Sarah, what *happened* out there?" she asked. "If you're not interested enough in the game to pay attention, why did you even sign up for sports?" She sighed and ran her hand through her hair. "Maybe you don't belong out here. Maybe you'd be more happy with your nose in a book," she muttered, and walked away.

Sarah felt like Abby had slapped her. For the rest of the game, she stood silent in left field, her eye never leaving the ball. David tried to joke around some more, but even he could tell that she wasn't in the mood. When the game finally ended—they lost, 8-6—David followed her off the field and touched her arm. "Hey," he said. "Sorry about that, Sarah."

Sarah just shook her head. "It's not your fault. I should have paid more attention." Ahead of her, she saw Abby shoot her another disgusted look and take off for the mess hall without waiting. The last two days, she'd at least been polite and waited to walk back with Sarah and Jenna.

David shrugged. "It's just a silly game. Don't beat yourself up."

Sarah sighed and nodded. *Right. Easy for you to say.*

Suddenly David leaned in close and took a big, loud, exaggerated sniff. "Hey," he said, leaning back and looking curiously into her eyes. "Is that *strawberry* I smell?" And then he smiled—a weird, smug smile—and ran off before Sarah could reply.

She stopped short on the ball field, watching him run. *What the heck was that about?* she wondered. *Just when you think boys might not be so weird . . .* Then it hit her. *Strawberry. Strawberry bug juice! The strawberry bug juice that was put in the showers the other day!* Sarah's mouth dropped open, and she started laughing in spite of herself. *They pranked us! David's bunk pranked ours!*

Sarah ran to 4C's table all ready to share her revelation, but the table was already buzzing. A bunch of 4A campers—Natalie, Tori, Jenna, and Chelsea—had come over to chat. Everyone was crowded around the four 4A girls, talking over one another and gesturing wildly. "Sarah!" Natalie said cheerfully as she approached the table. "Who are *you* going to the social with?"

Sarah felt her whole body sink. *The social. It's like I can't escape the stupid social.* She decided to dodge the question. "Aren't you guys mad at us?" she asked, looking at Natalie. "The last time I saw you, you were saying something about *karma?*"

Natalie smiled and shrugged. "That? I got over that *hours* ago. Right around the time I got back to the cabin with nine rolls of toilet paper. Bygones, you know?"

Sarah shook her head. "I dunno. You seemed upset this morning. Anyway, you're obviously going with Simon, right?"

Natalie blushed and smiled. "Duh."

"I have news," Brynn put in from the other side of the table, a big grin on her face.

"What's that?" asked Valerie.

Brynn's eyes lit up. She was always dramatic, and Sarah could tell she was enjoying being the center of attention. "Well, you know how in drama, I'm playing Annie and this cute guy named Darren is playing Daddy Warbucks? We've been flirting a lot more lately . . ."

A smile was forming on Tori's lips. "And . . . ?" she asked expectantly.

"And, well, today . . ." Brynn's cheeks were pink with happiness. "Today he asked me to be his date to the social!"

Sarah cringed as the table exploded in *oohs* and *ahhs*, especially from Natalie, Tori, and Alex. Sarah's stomach sank down to her feet. *Why didn't Brynn tell me about this guy before?* she wondered. *We used to talk about everything.*

"Congratulations!" Chelsea cried. "That's so great. Who's everyone else going with?"

"Do you guys know Geoff in 5G?" Alex asked.

"Sure," said Tori. "We're on the camp paper together. He's really nice."

Alex turned pink. "I think he's kind of cute."

"Oh, he *totally* is!" Tori agreed. "He's way cute, Alex. You should go for him."

Sarah had to struggle not to roll her eyes. *Go for*

him? What does that mean? Is there a big competition?

Alex was smiling, though. "I think I will." She looked down at the table for a minute, then seemed to remember something. "Oh! We're trying to get a real DJ for the social this year. We might have to cut down on the decorations, but we all thought it was important to have good music."

"And good lighting!" Brynn added. "Romantic. Soft. You know."

"Totally," Natalie agreed.

Sarah sighed and drummed her fingertips on the table. It was a shame this conversation was happening *before* dinner, because it was totally making her lose her appetite. Although after dinner, it might have made her lost her dinner altogether!

"Do you have anyone in mind to ask, Jenna?" Alex asked.

Jenna looked surprised by the question, but not as incredulous as Sarah might have expected. She didn't think Jenna had any interest in boys. But Jenna's answer surprised Sarah even more. She shrugged. "Maybe."

Alex's eyes widened. "Who?" she demanded Suddenly, Sarah couldn't take it anymore—she *had* to change the subject. And luckily, she had the perfect subject at hand.

"I almost forgot!" Sarah cried suddenly. "I was leaving sports today, and this guy David came up to me and was like"—she made an exaggerated sniff in the air—"'Hey, is that *strawberry* I smell?'"

Everyone at the table looked completely mystified.

"What?" Jenna asked finally.

Sarah rolled her eyes. "*David*, you know? Your brother's friend? Anyway, he made this big deal out of saying I smelled like *strawberry*. And then he had this weird smile. *Strawberry* is the flavor of bug juice that got put in our showerheads. Get it?"

Sarah looked around at her friends. They looked like she was speaking Martian. Nobody was getting it.

"*They* did it!" Sarah yelled. "David's bunk. Jenna was telling the truth. She never put bug juice in our showerheads! It was the boys! It was the boys all along!"

Everyone's mouth dropped open as the information slowly penetrated their brains.

"See!" Jenna cried after a few seconds. "I *told* you! I tried to tell you, like, a hundred times!"

"So you *were* telling the truth," Natalie said thoughtfully, turning to Jenna.

Jenna looked offended. "Of *course* I was. Why?"

Natalie gave a little embarrassed smile. "No offense," she said. "But up till now? I kind of thought there was a chance you really did it."

Jenna rolled her eyes. "Nobody trusts me."

"I don't get it," Abby spoke up suddenly. Everyone turned to look at her, surprised. "If the boys really pranked us, why would David just out and *tell* you? It doesn't make sense."

Sarah sighed. "It *does* make sense," she insisted. "That's how a prank war works."

"Why would David prank you guys?" Jenna suddenly spoke up. "He doesn't even *know* anyone in your whole bunk except you and Abby, right, Sarah?"

"Right," Sarah agreed slowly, thinking fast. "But it's not just him pranking us. It's his whole bunk. Maybe Adam said something to him?"

Jenna made a face. "Doubtful. I don't get it."

"I still don't think they necessarily did it," Abby spoke up. "I think the clue is weird. He said you smell like strawberries?"

Sarah nodded. "He said, 'Hey, is that—' "

Abby interrupted her. "Maybe he was just complimenting your shampoo, or something," she insisted. "Do you use strawberry shampoo?"

"No," Sarah said with a sigh. "I mean yes. Sometimes. But that isn't the point. Who smells someone's hair? He was *telling* me that they pranked us to take credit for the prank. What good is a one-sided prank war? We have to prank back."

Abby wasn't done arguing, though. "What good is a one-sided prank war? How about that you get away with it? How about that no one sneaks into your bunk in the middle of the night and steals all your toilet paper?"

"Word," Natalie muttered.

Sarah sighed again and sat up in her chair. "Abby. Listen. You're not helping here."

Abby looked offended. "I'm just trying to help figure this out."

"But you don't get it," Sarah explained. "Look, I've been coming here for years now. This is how a prank war works and how it's always worked. Okay?"

Abby started like Sarah had punched her. She blinked, then turned away. "*Oh*," she muttered. "Excuse *me*, then."

Sarah could tell she'd hurt Abby's feelings, but by the time she'd opened her mouth to apologize, everyone was talking at once.

"This is *huge*!" cried Alex. "I mean, the rivalry with 4A was one thing, but this is way huger."

"We have to get them back!" added Tiernan. "We can't let them get away with this. We pranked 4A this morning, and meanwhile the boys are running around scot-free!"

"This *is* big," agreed Jenna. "But . . . maybe you should let it go."

Everyone's mouth dropped open. *"What?!"* Sarah cried.

Jenna looked sheepish. "Look, I really don't want to get involved in any kind of prank war right now, all right?" She sighed. "I'm going back to our table. Whatever you plan, leave me out of it." She abruptly stood and walked back to the rest of 4A.

There was silence for a minute as everyone watched her go.

"I don't think you can let it go," Chelsea said slowly.

"Yeah?" Gaby asked. "It's serious, right? Whatever Jenna thinks. Does that mean you want to help us?"

Chelsea hesitated, then said, "Well. While I am *still* annoyed that you stole all of our toilet paper this morning, I think this outside attack is important enough that maybe we should put that aside."

Gaby beamed. "I agree totally." She looked around the table at the faces of all of the campers, looking more and more excited. "Ladies," she said, "I think we need to do something unprecedented here. An outsider has attacked one of our own. I think we need to form a two-bunk alliance."

"Two-bunk alliance?" Candace asked incredulously.

"Two-bunk alliance," Chelsea repeated with glee.

"Here's what we do," Gaby continued. "Since Jenna doesn't want to be involved, I think I should be the one to come up with the prank. And it's going to take some thought. This has to be, like, the best prank ever."

"What if we steal all their underwear and dump it in the lake?" Chelsea cried.

Gaby just gave her a withering look. "As I was saying," she said, "we need the prank to end all pranks. I'm going to think about it all night. When I've come up with something, I'll put out the word and we'll all meet in a secret location. We'll go over the plans there."

The CITs were beginning to come around with food, and Sarah could see Becky starting over to the table from the other side of the room. "All right," she agreed. "You guys had better get going. Dinner's starting."

Natalie, Tori, and Chelsea all got up. "See you," Nat called as they headed off.

"Bye," Sarah called back.

"Later," Gaby called after them with a secret smile. "I'll be in touch."

That night, Sarah decided to go on a night hike. It was an optional hike led by Derrick, one of the boys' counselors, through the forest without any flashlights. The idea was that after a while, your eyes adjust to the dark and you can see much more than you could with a flashlight. They walked down an easy trail, going slowly and being careful to feel the ground ahead of them with their feet. Sarah was amazed at how bright the moon and stars were. After they'd hiked a few minutes, and they were out of range of the camp lights, she realized it was true: She could see almost everything. The trees, the ground ahead of her, even the occasional owl. It was quiet and kind of beautiful. The stars never seemed quite this bright in Winthrop.

The hike finished up at the rec hall and Sarah thanked Derrick, then waited for Brynn, who'd also come along. Brynn was beaming as she joined up with Sarah for the walk back to the cabin. "Was that *incredible* or what? Have you ever seen so many stars?"

"Nope," Sarah agreed. "It was really cool."

Sarah kept trying to quiet her restless mind. All through the hike, she hadn't been able to stop thinking about Brynn and how she'd never mentioned Darren to her before. She'd tried to think about anything else— puppies, merry-go-rounds, David's stupid dance during the game that day. But nothing helped.

"Hey," Brynn said after a few minutes. "You're really quiet tonight. Is something up?"

Sarah shrugged. "No, I mean, not really. I dunno."

Brynn gave her a sympathetic look. "Jenna said you had a rough day in sports," she said. "Something about some dork in center field?"

Sarah shook her head. "That's not it," she said. She

took a deep breath. "Brynn, can I ask you something?"

Brynn looked surprised. "Sure."

"Why didn't you tell us about Darren until tonight?"

Brynn made a funny face, like that hadn't even occurred to her. "Well, Alex and Val and Candace and Grace already knew," she admitted. "I told them in the social-committee meeting. And you . . ." She looked uncomfortable all of a sudden. Sheepish—like she'd been caught in a lie.

"Me?" Sarah prompted.

"Well, you just . . ." Brynn looked really uncomfortable. "You seemed like you wouldn't want to hear about it, you know? I get the feeling you're sick of talking about the social. At all."

Sarah's face fell. She couldn't deny it—Brynn was right. She *was* sick of talking about the stupid dance. But she hated that it was separating her from some of her best friends in the world. With Abby around, she felt like she needed her friends more than ever, so the whole boy thing seemed even worse than it would have the year before. *Last year, I felt like everybody was like me,* Sarah thought. *What happened to all those people? What happened to all my friends?*

Brynn was still watching her, looking confused but sympathetic. Sarah could see that Brynn was honestly sorry for making her worry, but not sure what she'd done wrong.

"It's okay," Sarah said quickly, shaking her head. She didn't know what else to say. It *wasn't* okay, but how could she ever explain why without feeling like a freak or proving once and for all that she had nothing in common with her friends anymore? "You're right. I *am* tired of talking about it. In fact, I'm tired of everything right now. I can't wait to go to bed."

Brynn didn't look totally convinced, but she nodded and squeezed Sarah's shoulder as they entered the cabin. "Get some sleep, Sars," she agreed. "It will all look better in the morning. I promise."

"Right," Sarah murmured. She was quiet getting ready for bed, smiling at her bunkmates but not saying anything. When it was finally time for lights-out, she slipped into her sleeping bag eagerly. Then she stared at the springs above her for what seemed like hours, waiting for sleep to come.

SEVEN

A few mornings after Sarah's sleepless night, Chelsea shoved a note into her hand as she walked into breakfast. Sarah clutched it carefully, then opened it up as she and her bunkmates waited for Becky and Sophie to arrive.

"That's weird," Sarah murmured, staring at the marks on the paper.

"What's weird?" asked Gaby.

Sarah turned the paper over so everyone could see. "Chelsea just handed me this note, but there are no letters on it. It's all numbers."

"Let me see," said Abby, reaching across to take the note. Sarah handed it over, somewhat reluctantly. She and Abby had never discussed how Sarah had snapped at her about the prank war, or Sarah's big screwup during her first softball game. The last couple of days, Sarah had been playing *all right*—she'd hit a couple of balls and managed to avoid completely humiliating herself, but she hadn't earned any points or done anything spectacular. At least she hadn't earned any more sharp comments from Abby.

Abby flipped the note over and furrowed her

eyebrows. "It's a code," she said. "A simple code, actually. See?" She held up the note, and Sarah could see Chelsea's girly handwriting: $A=1$. $B=2$. *ETC.* Abby grabbed a pen from her pocket and scribbled the alphabet on top of the note. Then, above every letter, she wrote a number—1 for A, 2 for B, and so on. "Why would she send a note in code?"

"She must have been worried someone would intercept it," suggested Grace.

Abby rolled her eyes. "Let me guess," she said, with a sharp look at Sarah. "It's a *prank-war thing*?"

Sarah looked down at her hands.

Gaby frowned. "I *told* Chelsea I would come up with the prank," she muttered. "Why can't she be patient?"

Just then, Becky came over and sat down, greeting everyone with a cheery "Good morning." (Becky was such a morning person, Sarah found it kind of disgusting.) Abby held the note under the table and bent over it, scratching in the letters. By the time Sophie came by with eggs and bacon, Abby had translated the whole thing. She passed it around to each camper under the table. Sarah got the note last and bent down to read it while Becky was deep in a conversation with Grace.

ALL OF 4C: MEET ME AT THE BIG OAK TREE OUTSIDE OUR CABIN AT 1600 HOURS, the note said. Sarah knew military time from her dad—1600 hours was four in the afternoon. MAKE SURE YOU ARE NOT FOLLOWED. C.

Sarah glanced up at Gaby and raised her eyebrows. This was going to be interesting.

In sports that morning, the Tigers were playing Jenna's team, the Bears. Sarah was still stuck in left field, having to try extra-hard to pay attention when she was really bored and worried that the ball would never come to her again. David tried to clown around and get her attention, but she just smiled and turned back to the game. David was nice and all, but she was *not* going to let him ruin this for her. She still had faith that she could turn this around and start acting like the amazing athlete she knew she was.

It was kind of weird playing against Jenna's team, though. All this time Sarah had felt bad about playing badly with just Abby and David watching. Having Jenna around added a whole new layer of pressure. Jenna had actually seen Sarah at her best and was probably wondering what was going on. *And unfortunately, I don't have any answers*, Sarah mused with a sigh.

"All right, Tigers, let's turn this around!" Abby yelled as she struck one of the Bears out and ended the eighth inning. The Bears were leading, 3-2. "I want to see some super batting out there! I expect everyone to do their best!"

Sarah trotted slowly out of left field and over to the bench that was acting as dugout. She had to admit, over the last couple of days, she had noticed that Abby was actually a good team captain. She had her bossy moments, but that only seemed to annoy Sarah and David. She inspired the team—at least, all the team members other than Sarah, who was still just praying for the opportunity to show her up—but didn't put so much pressure on them that they choked up at bat or on the field. *Yeah, I'm the only one who chokes up around here,* thought Sarah. *And when you choke up, suddenly Abby's not so nice.*

David was first up at bat. He walked up to home plate and began swinging the bat around, loosening up his arms. For all of his goofiness, David was actually a great batter and a decent outfielder, when he paid attention. *He's able to just relax and have fun,* Sarah thought. *I should do more of that.* As David made strike one, she tried to loosen up her shoulders and be less stressed out. *It's just a game. It's just a game. It's just a game.*

David hit the next ball and got to first base. Lily, a quiet girl from 4B, was up after him, and after a few foul balls she got a single, too. Then came Sheldon, a moppy-haired kid from 5F. He hit a fly ball to center field and got an out. After him came Kelly, who got a single, and then Jimmy, who struck out. *Omigod,* Sarah thought suddenly as she stood up to bat. *Bases loaded. Two outs. And I'm up.*

"Come on, Sarah!" she heard Jenna scream from her spot as third baseman. "You can do it! Hit it over the fence!"

Sarah felt the waves of confusion moving through Jenna's team members as they wondered why she was cheering someone from the opposite team. *She just feels bad for me,* she thought. *She knows I've been messing up so much, I'll really be crushed if I mess this up, too.* Sarah started to feel heavy all over as she reached home plate. All of the relaxation she'd felt on the bench left her, and she felt herself tense up.

"Come on, Sarah," Abby yelled encouragingly. "Show us what a great player you really are!"

Sarah picked up the bat and tried to make a few

practice swings. She didn't feel loose at all, and her swings were too fast and jerky. *Calm down*, she told herself. *Calm down! Calm DOWN!* But the more she willed herself to relax, the less relaxed she felt. It was like she was one of those puppets on a string, and someone was pulling all of her strings tight so her limbs locked.

"Ready?" the pitcher called, winding up.

"Ready," Sarah said, but she was thinking, *Ready as I'm gonna get.* The ball flew toward her, and Sarah tried to line up the bat. *Come on! Hit it!* She swung, but missed by a mile.

"Strike one!" yelled Kimberly.

The ball was thrown back to the pitcher, who wound up again and waited for Sarah to get over home plate. Sarah stood there, desperately trying to loosen up, but her limbs felt like they were made of ice, and her heart was pounding a mile a minute. "Go, Sarah!" Jenna yelled again from third base. *She knows*, Sarah thought. *She knows I'm freaking out.*

The pitcher let go of the ball, and it seemed to come toward Sarah in slow motion. Desperately, she swung.

"Strike two!" yelled Kimberly.

"Come on, Sarah," Abby yelled again. She was trying to sound encouraging, but Sarah could hear the annoyance in her voice. "Last chance. You can do it!"

This is it, Sarah told herself. *If you make a hit, we'll probably win. If not, we'll lose and everyone will blame you.* She stretched her shoulders and tried again to loosen up, but she still felt tense and jerky. Her heart was pounding so loud, she thought the outfielders must be able to hear it.

She swung the bat to her shoulder and stood over home plate, trying to look more prepared than she felt.

Sarah saw the ball leave the pitcher's glove, but she didn't see it sail by her. She was busy swinging with all her might. "Strike three!" yelled Kimberly. "That's three outs! Sorry, Tigers—the Bears win!"

Sarah dropped the bat as the Bears erupted in cheers, moving around to slap each other five and give hugs. The Tigers were silent. When she turned around, Abby was scowling. She got off the bench and walked up close to Sarah, close enough that nobody else could hear what she was saying.

"What's with you?" she hissed. She turned on her heel and stomped off before Sarah could respond.

I failed, Sarah thought miserably. *Again. I'm never going to show her that I'm a great athlete, too.*

David came running over from third base and patted her on the back. "No sweat, Sarah," he reassured her. "What's one more off day? When you have a good day, it's going to blow everyone's socks off. *I* believe you're a great athlete."

Sarah sighed. "Well, I'm glad," she told him, "because I'm starting to not believe it myself."

David looked confused. "Whaddaya mean?"

Sarah shrugged. "Maybe I never was that great an athlete, you know? I mean, I didn't play last session, and I'm *so* awful this session. What if I was never that great?"

Jenna ran up just in time to hear the last part. "Never that great?" she asked, moving in between David and Sarah. "What are you *talking* about? You're awesome, Sars, and everybody knows it."

Sarah just looked at the ground, shaking her head. "Then why can't I *play* awesome?" She started walking back to the mess hall, leaving Jenna and David gaping behind her.

▲ ▲ ▲

Four o'clock fell during free time, so all of 4C met up in front of their cabin and walked over to the oak tree in front of 4A together. Everyone else was chattering excitedly, but Sarah had been in a deep funk ever since sports that morning. *Maybe I am exactly like Abby thinks I am—quiet and shy, not athletic at all. Maybe there's only one Sarah Peyton: the Sarah I am at home. Maybe I should stop trying to be something I'm not.*

Chelsea was sitting on a low branch of the tree, with the girls of 4A scattered around her. The 4C girls walked over and settled down. Sarah sat on the ground with Alex, Brynn, Valerie, and Grace, noting that Jenna was nowhere to be seen.

"But purple is a *much* better color for decorations!" Valerie was saying. "I like yellow, too, but it's just not a dance-y color."

"Dancey schmancy," replied Alex. "It'll look great in the dark."

"Who said it'll be dark?" asked Brynn. "We asked them to make it darker, but they haven't told us yet whether they will."

Just then, Chelsea stood up. "Hey, everyone," she greeted them. "4C, I'm glad you understood my note. I apologize for the code. But I couldn't risk anyone discovering my plans." Suddenly she looked left and right, searching the woods for intruders. "Does anyone think she might have been followed here?"

Natalie looked at her like she was nuts. "Chelsea?" she asked. "Are you feeling all right?"

Chelsea looked back at her and seemed to recover. "I'm fine," she replied. "We have to take this seriously, guys. A three-bunk war is a serious thing. We have to hit them hard before they catch on to our alliance."

"So?" Gaby spoke up. "Let's get to it, then. What's the *plan*, Chelsea? It must be a good one, since you couldn't wait for me to come up with mine."

Chelsea's face flooded with pride. "Oh, it is. In fact, it's the best darn prank plan this camp has ever seen!" she replied.

"Let's hear it," called Alex.

"Yeah," Tori agreed. "Let's get this show on the road. I wanted to paint my toenails this free period."

Chelsea sighed, looking annoyed by their impatience, and sat back down on the branch. "All right," she began. "What we do is . . ."

What followed was the most elaborate prank Sarah had ever heard of. Everyone fell dead silent, listening to Chelsea describe each step in perfect detail. Sarah couldn't deny that if they pulled it off, it would be a fantastic prank. But it didn't sound completely fantastic the way Chelsea was telling it. It sounded . . . risky.

"See?" Chelsea said as she reached the end of the plan. "We'll get them *so* good. Ladies, this is the prank to end all pranks. So who's in?" She stopped and beamed proudly at all the assembled campers.

There was dead silence as all the girls turned to

get the reactions of the people sitting next to them. Sarah turned to Alex and Valerie. They looked just as unconvinced as Sarah felt. Then she looked over at some of the 4A girls. They, too, looked surprised and concerned—Alyssa was slowly shaking her head at Nat.

"Come on!" Chelsea encouraged them. "Don't be shy. It's a great prank!"

It was quiet for a few seconds more. "Um," Grace finally spoke up. "It would be a great prank, Chelsea, no doubt about it. *If* we could pull it off. It sounds kind of . . . risky."

"Risky?" asked Chelsea in surprise.

All of the campers started nodding. "No offense," Karen spoke up, "but if we get caught, we could be in serious trouble. And we'd be out there long enough . . . it just seems like it would be really easy for something to go wrong and all of us get caught."

Chelsea looked amazed that the group wasn't totally in love with her plan. "But I thought of that!" she protested. "That's why we dress all in black. So no one sees us!"

"Dressing all in black doesn't make you invisible," Alex muttered, loud enough to be heard. The other campers murmured their agreement. Chelsea looked around the crowd, totally taken aback.

"Listen," she said. "I only need three people to pull this off. And I have total faith in this prank, so I'll be one of them." She looked from camper to camper. "Who's with me?"

Everything was totally quiet. Sarah felt a little bad—she was the one who'd brought up the whole *boys* thing, and now it looked like Chelsea was going to get revenge alone. Still, the prank *did* sound risky. And if she volunteered and got caught, the camp would be sure to call her parents. Sarah *hated* getting in trouble.

"I'll do it," Gaby suddenly spoke up behind her. Chelsea tried to keep her cool, but Sarah could see the relief on her face. "It does sound like a great prank," Gaby went on. "I'll give you that. I'm in."

"Awesome!" Chelsea beamed. She looked back at the assembled campers, sweeping her eyes over the crowd. "I've got two. I only need one more—*one* brave volunteer. Who's with me?" Sarah felt a little chill as Chelsea's eyes met hers. It seemed like such a bad idea . . . and yet . . .

Sarah turned to her left, where Abby was sitting with Gaby. Gaby was anxiously searching the crowd, looking just as tense as Chelsea. She kept giving meaningful glances to Abby, but Abby looked torn. She kept looking at Chelsea, then looking around at everyone else's reaction. *She would do it*, Sarah realized. *But she's scared. She wants to, but she's afraid of getting in trouble.*

Sarah didn't even feel her arm go up in the air. She was barely aware of announcing to the crowd, "I'll do it, too." But as soon as the words were out of her mouth, people were turning to her in surprise, and Chelsea was getting up with a huge smile and running over to her.

"Awesome!" Chelsea cried. "You won't regret this, Sarah, I promise. We'll get David's bunk so good, they won't know what hit them!"

Right, Sarah thought. *Kind of like I don't know what hit me right now. Or what got into me.* But then she felt Abby's eyes on her and turned to face her. Abby looked surprised, but also something else—something much better. Yes, Sarah was sure of it: There was *jealousy* in her eyes. Abby wished that she had been the one to volunteer for the final space. And now she was too late.

For the first time that she could remember at camp this summer, Sarah felt totally satisfied.

chapter
EIGHT

Dear Diane,

Thanks for your letter. I'm glad
you had such an awesome time at Lake
Winnipesaukee this year! I wish I'd been able
to go with you, but camp's finally looking up.
Abby and I are in sports together, which
is not going anything like I planned it. But
what I'm really excited about is, we're having
a prank war with a boys' bunk—there's this
kid, David, in sports with me and for some
reason his bunk pranked us. They put bug
juice in our showerheads a few days ago—so
gross! But Chelsea's got this awesome prank

planned to get him back. I could tell Abby wanted to volunteer to help, but somehow I got my hand up first...

"Hey." Grace was smiling down at Sarah when she looked up from her letter. "Ready to swim?"

"Ready." Sarah smiled. It was the end of siesta, but she'd actually just returned to the cabin a few minutes before. She'd been busy with Chelsea and Gaby, carrying out Stage One of the Big Prank.

Sarah put aside her letter and got up from her bunk. It was a beautiful day, warmer than usual, with a nice breeze off the lake. All of her bunkmates got into their bathing suits and collected in front of the cabin, then started the short walk to the lake together. As soon as they'd gotten away from the cabin, the bunkmates converged on Gaby and Sarah.

"So . . . how'd it go?" Brynn whispered.

"Yeah," Candace said. "How'd it go?"

"It went *fine*," Gaby replied. "Keep your voices down."

"Did anyone see you?" asked Tiernan. "Did anyone ask you what was in the bags?"

"No," whispered Gaby.

"It was simple, really," Sarah added. "Just moving things from one place to the other."

"I know," Abby put in, staring straight ahead. "Seriously, guys, it's not like it was a big deal."

As they reached the lake, Sarah couldn't help smiling. *She's so jealous,* she thought with satisfaction.

I'm so glad I volunteered for this prank. Finally, something I have over Abby!

"It *was* a big deal!" Grace broke in. "If they got caught, they'd be in big trouble."

Abby rolled her eyes, looking away from the group, out at the lake. "Anybody want to race me to the dock?"

"I know," Candace agreed, ignoring Abby. "You guys are brave to do this. It's so cool that you pulled the first part off."

Gaby grinned. "I know," she agreed. "And I hate to admit it, but Chelsea really did come up with a great prank. If you think it's cool now, just wait till we pull the rest of it off."

Abby made a face like she'd smelled something awful. "Aren't we here to *swim*, not talk about the prank?"

"I could never do it," Valerie whispered, not paying any attention to Abby. "Honestly, I don't know how you guys did it without freaking out. You must have nerves of steel."

Suddenly, Abby turned from the lake and faced Sarah, looking royally annoyed. "You know," she said, "it's funny about that. I'm really surprised you volunteered for this, Sars. At school you're not exactly a risk-taker."

Sarah was stunned. *This is it,* she thought. *She's going to tell them all that I'm some kind of lame-o at school. My cover will be blown.* "Well—uh—" she stammered. "I love a great prank. I mean, I've always loved a great prank."

"What do you mean, she's not a risk-taker at school?" Gaby asked, smiling a little at the new gossip. "What's Sarah like at school? Tell us. I'm curious."

Abby smiled, looking pleased to be the center of

attention. "Well," she said. "It's nothing bad. She's just . . . different."

"Different how?" Alex asked, looking skeptical.

Abby shrugged. "Quieter. Smart. All the teachers love her."

Gaby's smile grew and became meaner. "You mean she's a nerd?"

Sarah's heart sank. It was the meanest thing anyone could possibly say about her, and there it was, *out* there. The word she hated more than any other.

Abby suddenly looked uncomfortable. She looked out at the lake again. "I didn't say that," she said quickly. "Just . . . quiet and smart. She kind of keeps to herself." She glanced at Sarah and seemed to get more annoyed. "Like, she doesn't spend all her time flirting at home."

Sarah's mouth dropped open at that one.

"*Flirting?*" Alex asked with a laugh. "*Sarah?* What are you talking about?"

"Yeah," Brynn agreed with a chuckle. "If there's one thing we *know* about Sarah, it's that she's not 'into' boys."

Abby frowned at Sarah, like she thought Sarah was holding back information or something. "All I know is what I see," she replied. "And in sports, Sarah, you spend *all* your time flirting with that David kid."

Sarah let out a short bark of laughter. "*David?!*" she cried. "*Flirting?* You think I'm *flirting* with David?"

Abby shrugged. "What would you call it?" she asked. "All I know is, every time I look at the outfield, you two are out there laughing it up and doing cartwheels or whatever."

"No, no no no no no," Sarah insisted. "David does

cartwheels and whatever. He does something ridiculous, and I look it him like, you're ridiculous, and then the ball comes at me and I miss it. Is that flirting?"

Abby threw her hands up, looking really annoyed now. "Call it whatever you want, Sars. It looks like flirting to me. It's sure not *catching the ball*, and that's all I care about." Abby stomped off to the lake, leaving the group. Everyone watched as she waded into the lake and started swimming out to the area for advanced swimmers. Then the bunkmates turned to Sarah in stunned silence.

"Sarah and David, sittin' in a tree . . ." Gaby cooed.

Sarah rolled her eyes. "That's so far from the truth, it's actually funny."

"So there's no truth to it?" Alex asked curiously. "Really? You don't like him at all?"

"I like him *as a friend*," Sarah said. "A little. I guess. But Abby's way off."

Brynn shrugged, dropping her towel on the ground. "Well, one thing's clear," she told Sarah with a mischievous grin. "*Somebody* better start concentrating on the ball." All of Sarah's bunkmates laughed as Brynn ran over to the dock and dove into the water.

▲ ▲ ▲

Sitting on the bench in sports the next morning, Sarah couldn't help giggling whenever she thought of what Abby had said. Imagine, she and David, having some kind of stupid romance out in the outfield! *If David ever tried to kiss me*, Sarah thought, *I'd punch him. Twice.* She couldn't believe Abby had really thought that was what was going on out there.

"Sarah!" Abby suddenly appeared in front of her. "You're next up at bat. Get ready! Look alive." Abby ran back behind home plate to watch Jimmy bat, and Sarah shook her head and got to her feet. She'd actually been doing okay lately. Not awful, and not great. Just okay. She'd caught a couple balls in left field, and hit the ball more often than she struck out. It gave her back a little of her confidence. For the moment, at least, Abby had nothing to complain about.

The Tigers were playing the Bears again. Both teams were doing pretty well in the tournament—right now, they were the top two. Jimmy hit a double and ran to second base. Sarah picked up the bat he had thrown down and swung it a few times, feeling its weight in her arms.

When she was ready, she walked up and stood over home plate. She caught Jenna's eye at third base, and Jenna just waved and smiled. Sarah smiled back, thinking of what Abby had said again. She couldn't help laughing a little. The ball came toward her, but it was too high to swing at. "Ball one," announced Kimberly.

The pitcher warmed up a little, then wound up and threw a knuckleball. Sarah watched it curve easily through the air and toward her bat. Without even thinking about it, she swung, and heard the sharp *crack* of the ball ricocheting off her bat. It soared into the air, past second base, past the center fielder—and *over the fence!*

"Home run!" yelled Kimberly. "Great job, Sarah!

That's three points for your team! It puts you in the lead, 5-3!"

Sarah just stood there in openmouthed shock. Kimberly had to yell to her: "Run, Sarah! You have to run the bases!"

"Oh!" Sarah cried, coming out of her stupor and jerking toward first base. "Right!"

Jenna was laughing as Sarah approached third, and clapped her on the back. "Awesome job, Sarah! That's the girl I know!"

When Sarah ran back to home, all of her teammates had gotten off the bench and ran forward to hug her or slap her five. "Great job!" Lily said.

"I knew you could do it," added Kelly.

David ran forward with a huge smile. "I guess you *are* a Curt Schilling!" he said.

Sarah started laughing. "Well, sometimes I am."

David nodded. "Great job, buddy." He leaned in and, before Sarah could think anything about it, gave her a hug. It felt so natural, Sarah hugged him back warmly. But then she remembered what Abby had said. *Uh-oh,* Sarah thought. *What is he doing? Does everyone think we're flirting?*

Just then, another pair of arms were thrown around her from behind, and Sarah turned around to see Jenna's smiling face. "I ran in from third base just for a second," she said. "I just wanted to hug you, too."

David heard that and, laughing, threw an arm around Jenna. He, Sarah, and Jenna all cracked up in their three-person hug until finally David let go.

Sarah couldn't stop beaming. She couldn't remember the last time she felt this totally happy. Then all of a sudden, she realized: Where was Abby? She turned around and around to look for her, but it was a minute or so before she located her: sitting on the grass off to the side, totally on her own. Everyone else on the team was still cheering for Sarah. But Abby, the person who should be most excited, wasn't—she was scowling at her.

chapter
NINE

Sarah lay in her bunk, staring at the springs above her. But this time, she wasn't worrying herself awake—she was waiting. Tonight was the night: the prank to end all pranks. And Sarah was going to be part of it.

She kept checking her watch until a full hour had gone by after lights-out. Then she lay very still and listened. Everyone else seemed to be asleep. Sarah sat up and nodded at Gaby, then they slipped silently out of their bunks—something Sarah was getting very good at—and tiptoed over to the door in their black T-shirts and sweatpants. Sarah had wanted to wear her Red Sox hat for luck, but Chelsea had explained that that would only make it easier to identify her if they were spotted.

Chelsea was waiting by the oak tree outside 4A's cabin. Sarah's whole body seemed to be tingling with excitement. Or was that fear? She really did think this was a great prank, but if they got caught, it would be big trouble for all of them. *Definitely* calls to their parents—and maybe, depending on how the camp director was feeling, a session with no activities.

"Ready?" Chelsea whispered when Sarah and Gaby approached.

"Ready," Sarah replied.

"Ready," Gaby echoed.

Silently, they began the hike to 4E's cabin.

A week before, Chelsea had overheard two counselors talking. One was saying that 4E's counselor, Kenny, had tonight off and was planning to go into town. The other counselor had thought it was funny because whenever Kenny was gone, the CIT, a friend of hers, slipped off by the lake to meet his girlfriend, who was also a CIT. The counselors had just been joking about it, but to Chelsea, it meant only one thing: 4E was unguarded tonight. At least, it was unguarded until midnight or so, when the CIT usually slipped back in. That meant opportunity. Bunk 4E was a cabin just waiting to be pranked.

The girls didn't speak at all, or use flashlights, because they were afraid of being spotted. That made the hike very quiet and longer than usual. Sarah had plenty of time to psych herself up. *I bet Abby wishes she could be here,* she thought. *I bet she's never been so jealous in her entire life.*

Finally the cabin came into sight. Chelsea held up her hand and they all stopped while she handed them something to put on: black masquerade masks. Something her parents had sent when Chelsea told them the social committee was considering a masquerade theme for the camp social. Also very handy for those who don't want to be recognized.

Once the masks were on, Chelsea led the way to the cluster of trees where they'd hidden the garbage bags. Very carefully, they pulled out one of them. With the bag at their feet, they paused and looked at one another.

"Ready?" Chelsea whispered.

"Ready," Sarah affirmed.

"Ready," Gaby whispered.

Chelsea clutched the handle of the bag. "One . . . two . . . three . . . GO!"

They ran to the door of 4E's cabin, and Chelsea threw it open with a loud *bang*. As the boys began rousing from their beds and muttering "What the . . ." Chelsea, Sarah, and Gaby each reached into the garbage bags and pulled out several balloons. Before the boys could react, they began throwing, and soon the air was filled with shrieks and yells and the satisfying *sploosh* of a water balloon hitting its target.

"*Aaaaaahhh!*" Sarah heard Jenna's brother Adam yell. "It's gotta be my sister's little friends! They're getting revenge for the bug juice!"

"*No mercy!*" Chelsea screamed. She grabbed three balloons and flung them, one by one, at Adam's head.

Sarah threw balloons at every moving target. She saw David rouse from his top bunk and immediately hunker back down under his sleeping bag. Soon the whole bunk was soaked, and half of the boys looked like drowned rats in their dripping-wet pajamas. The shouts continued—"*Augh!*" "Stop!" "Not at the beds!"—but so did the attack.

After what seemed like hours, but was probably only a few seconds, Chelsea fished the last balloon out of the garbage bag. "Justice!" she yelled, aiming it at David's head. It exploded all over his sleeping bag, and he groaned. "That'll teach you to mess with girls from the fourth division!" Then, just as quickly as they had come, they grabbed the garbage bags and darted off into the night. They ran over to the trees where they had stashed the garbage bags and waited.

All three girls were struggling to stifle their giggles.

"That was *awesome!*" Chelsea whispered.

Gaby shook her head in delight. "It couldn't have gone better," she whispered back.

Sarah was beaming, still on a high from the amazingly successful first wave. "It was perfect," she whispered. "Maybe . . . too perfect." She could hear the boys talking loudly in the cabin, complaining and wondering who exactly had planned the prank. "What if we just left now?" she whispered.

The voices in the boys' cabin were getting louder, and they sounded pretty angry.

Chelsea looked at Sarah like she'd suggested maybe ice cream was too bad for you to eat and TV would give you cancer. "Are you *crazy?*" she hissed. "Sarah, that's the whole beauty of this prank. The second wave. See"—here she started giggling hysterically—"they think it's over, but it's *not!* Because we go back!"

As she always did at this point in the explanation, Chelsea doubled over, giggling, and Sarah and Gaby had to wait for her to recover. "We go *back!*" Chelsea whispered, throwing herself into another fit of giggles.

"I get it," Sarah whispered. "And it's great. It's a great prank. But maybe . . . just because the first wave went so incredibly well . . . we should quit while we're ahead?"

"*No quitting!*" Chelsea hissed. "It's only the perfect prank *as planned*. And don't we need the perfect prank here? Don't we? Gaby?" She looked at her friend for help.

"I'm with Chelsea," Gaby agreed. Sarah expected that, because Gaby had been weirdly gung-ho about the whole prank thing lately. The voices from the boys' cabin were calming down. Chelsea reached in and pulled out one garbage bag, then another. Silently, she pushed one bag at Gaby, then grabbed the handle of the other one.

"Good thing Tiernan had a birthday last week," Sarah whispered. "Her parents had no trouble sending all these balloons."

"Stop stalling," Chelsea whispered. "Ready, ladies?"

"Ready," said Gaby quickly.

Sarah waited for a minute, looking around the peaceful woods and taking a deep breath. "Ready," she said finally.

Chelsea nodded. "One . . . two . . . three . . . GO!"

They dashed over to the cabin door, albeit a little slower than last time, since they were dragging an extra bag of water balloons. Chelsea grabbed the door handle. With a mighty bellow, she flung it open—

WHAP! WHAP! WHAP! SPLOOSH!

Sarah was smacked on the head with two water balloons, and then suddenly her legs were soaking wet.

WHAP! SPLOOSH! WHAP! SPLOOSH!

"They're throwing water balloons at *us*!" Gaby shrieked. "How is that possible?"

"Don't worry about it!" Chelsea yelled. "Just get them back!"

Sarah, Gaby, and Chelsea all flung the balloons

they were holding into the cabin. A couple broke, but Sarah was stunned to see David *catch* one in midair and hurl it back at Chelsea's feet, where it landed with a *sploosh*.

"The unbroken ones!" Sarah cried. "They must have collected the unbroken ones last time to throw at us this time!"

"But how is that possible?" Gaby demanded, digging deep into the garbage bag and flinging three balloons at once. "How did they know we were coming back?"

"Simple!" Adam yelled, catching one of the balloons and bombing Chelsea with it. "David and I followed you back into the woods! We heard about your *perfect* plan—the prank to end all pranks!" He laughed loudly.

Gaby moaned as another balloon hit her shoulder and exploded in her face. "This is *horrible!*" she cried. "Let's get out of here!" She flung the last two balloons in her garbage bag and ran out. Chelsea threw the last balloon in her bag, then quickly followed her. Sarah dashed after them.

But the door didn't shut behind them. It whacked against the door frame several times as it opened to let out a horde of wet, angry boys. "Get them!" Adam yelled. "We can't let them get away with this!"

Sarah, Gaby, and Chelsea were all running as fast as they could. Sarah's lungs were burning.

"Split up!" cried Chelsea. "We'll meet up back at the cabins. We'll have better luck on our own!"

Chelsea took off to the left, Gaby took off to the right, and Sarah ran straight. She darted between trees, changed direction, and tried to fake the boys out. But no matter what she did, she couldn't shake the sound of footsteps behind her. *Somebody* was still following her. At least she had a good lead.

She ran by the lake, past the boathouse, toward the swamp. Then she darted back into the woods, ran past the infirmary, and back into the trees. The footsteps were getting farther in the distance. Sarah started to slow down—and then suddenly her foot caught on something, and she was sailing forward.

She reached out to catch herself just before her face hit the tree stump, but she still got the wind knocked out of her lungs. She'd scraped her knee and her ankle hurt again. For a few seconds, she just lay there, trying to catch her breath. And then . . . the footsteps came back. They were approaching her, slower now. *Oh no!* thought Sarah. *I'm caught! They'll tell my parents! I'll be in so much trouble!* For a minute, Sarah recalled very clearly why she never got involved in crazy schemes at home. She twisted her body and tried to get up, but her ankle ached and she couldn't move fast enough. Before she knew it, a dark shape was standing over her.

"Caught," came David's voice.

"You!" Sarah turned around and sat on the ground facing him. "Please, David, we're friends, right? Let me go. You know I wasn't out to hurt anybody. It was just in good fun. You know?"

"*Fun?*" David asked. "You guys nailed me *in the face* with a water balloon! How was that fun for me?"

Sarah shrugged. "I dunno. But you got me, too! It's a prank war! These things happen."

David raised an eyebrow. "Yeah? What do *you* think I should do with you?"

Sarah didn't hesitate. "Let me go. We'll both pretend this never happened."

David grinned. "Really. Because, you know, Doug, our CIT, is probably back by now. I think I should bring you to our cabin and let him figure it out."

"*No!*" Sarah cried. "Please, David! No counselors! You know they'd call our parents."

"Maybe they *should* call your parents," David said, crossing his arms. "That was pretty messed-up behavior. Breaking curfew. Breaking and entering. Destroying camp property."

"*Destroying?*" Sarah gave him a doubtful look.

"Well, getting it wet." David shrugged. "Either way, it's bad news. *You're* bad news, Sarah Peyton."

Sarah shook her head furiously. "But I'm not! Really, I am *so* not. I'm the nicest, most normal person. Quiet. A total teacher's pet."

"Really?" David asked. "Then why are you acting crazy here?"

Sarah took a deep breath. She shrugged. "I dunno," she admitted. "Maybe I like having the freedom to be different at camp." She gestured back to the cabin. "To act crazy, like tonight."

David shook his head. "I don't know, that sounds dangerous," he said. "How do I know you won't act crazy again? Besides, I'd be betraying my whole bunk if I let you go. I'd better turn you in."

Sarah looked up at him, right into his eyes. She sighed. He had a point, and she couldn't say for sure that she wouldn't do the same thing if the roles were reversed. Still, it just . . . stunk. She reluctantly got to her feet. *My parents are going to be so mad.*

"Let's go," said David. He took a few steps toward the boys' cabins, and she followed him. *I don't believe this,* she was thinking. *I almost got away. I was so close.*

She almost didn't notice that David had stopped again and was smiling at her. She almost walked into him, then looked up, confused. "What's up?" she asked. "Why are we stopping?"

David shrugged and looked away from her, out over the lake. "Tell you what," he said. "Let's say I let you go this one time. But you owe me."

Sarah felt a smile creep across her whole face. "Of course, David! Just let me go, and I'll be soooo grateful!"

David looked at her carefully, smiling faintly, and nodded. "All right," he agreed. "You owe me. Be careful walking back, Sarah. And stay out of trouble."

The whole way back to the cabin, Sarah planned in her head how she would describe what happened to Gaby and Chelsea. *And then . . . he just let me go. And he had this funny smile. And then . . .*

As she came out of the woods, she spotted the two of them sitting on the oak tree. She ran over to them with a big smile. "Hey!"

They looked up at her curiously. "Hey yourself," Chelsea replied. "I guess the prank to end all pranks didn't quite go as planned. It was close for me, getting back, but I think I lost Adam when I ran underneath a low branch."

"Yeah," Gaby agreed. "I had trouble, too. But I just finally got enough distance between us, whoever was following me gave up."

"Yeah," Chelsea agreed.

"Yeah," said Sarah.

There was silence for a minute. Gaby and Chelsea both looked at Sarah expectantly. "How about you?" Chelsea asked finally. "Sarah, did you have any trouble?"

Sarah looked into Chelsea's face, trying to compose the words. She didn't know why she was having so much trouble figuring out what to tell her friends. *David followed me. And he caught me. But then . . . he let me go . . . I don't know why . . .*

"No," she said after a moment.

"Good," said Chelsea. She stood up from the tree and brushed herself off. "Well, ladies, it's been a long night, and I don't know about you, but I'm pretty wet."

"Me too," agreed Gaby.

"Me too," added Sarah.

"I think it's time to get some dry pajamas on and slip into bed." Chelsea stretched and let out a sigh.

"Sounds good to me," agreed Sarah.

"Me too," said Gaby.

"Thanks for your help, guys," Chelsea said with a wry smile. "I'm sorry it didn't go as planned. But you guys were great."

"So were you, Chelsea," Sarah assured her, patting her back.

"Oh well," said Chelsea. "We'll got 'em pretty good the first time. Good night."

"Good night."

"Good night."

Sarah walked slowly back to her bunk, savoring the cool night air and the smell of the lake and the trees. In her cabin, she quietly pulled out her pajamas and went into the bathroom to change. She stowed her black clothes in her cubby and got into her sleeping bag with a big yawn.

Sarah didn't know why, but she couldn't get this big smile off her face.

chapter TEN

In sports the next day, Sarah continued playing like the great athlete she thought she was. She hit a triple and made a game-saving catch. Her team members were starting to take notice of her talents, and it felt great.

"Nice job!" Kelly told her after her triple sent in a run.

Abby, who was standing right behind Kelly, had to either say something or risk looking rude. "Yeah," she echoed under her breath. "Nice job, Sars."

Sarah didn't understand why her *finally* playing well didn't have Abby jumping up and down for joy, but she wasn't going to question it. *Maybe she's jealous,* she thought. *I know what that feels like. Besides, I have enough people telling me how great I am—what's one who doesn't?*

She didn't get much chance to talk to David during the game, since she was concentrating so hard on her playing. But after the game ended, he came up to her and slapped her five. "Awesome job, Peyton," he told her. "I knew you had it in you."

"You did, huh?" Sarah grinned.

"Sure I did." David glanced at her out of the corner of his eye. "Really, Sarah. You're really talented."

Sarah looked over in surprise, but David wasn't looking at her. He was staring at the ground, like he'd found some really fascinating rock.

"Thanks, David," she said. "That's a really nice thing to say. And thanks again for—" She looked around to see if anyone was listening. She didn't see anyone, but she lowered her voice anyway. "—for letting me go last night."

David shrugged. "It's no biggie." He paused and looked around him. They'd walked away from most of the crowd and were on a quiet path back to the mess hall. "Um, Sarah," he said quietly, making Sarah turn back.

"What?" she asked.

He looked up at her, and suddenly Sarah noticed that his eyes were a really pretty shade of green. Like the moss they found in the forest, with a little yellow thrown in. Suddenly, he looked all serious. Sarah opened her mouth to say something, not sure whether she wanted to hear what he had to say.

But he beat her anyway. "I was thinking about something."

Sarah frowned at him, skeptical. She wasn't sure she'd ever seen him be serious before. "Um, okay. What's that?"

All trace of a smile left his face and suddenly David looked a little scared. "Maybe you could go to the social with me."

Sarah was so stunned, she didn't respond right away. She felt her mouth drop open and just left her lower lip hanging there while she thought this over. *He wants to go to the stupid social with me? Why? Since when? Does that mean he—could it mean he—*

"I really like you, Sarah."

Omigod. Omigod. Omigod. Punch him.

Sarah was so confused, she halfheartedly raised her right hand to punch but quickly dropped it.

I don't think I want to.

"And I hear the social's going to be pretty cool. They're bringing in a DJ and decorating all in purple or something. Anyway, I thought it would be really fun if we could just hang out together. We don't have to, like, dance or anything. We could just hang out by the punch bowl and drink punch."

"I don't like punch," Sarah said. It was true, but it was not something she planned to say, and she wasn't sure what she meant by it.

"Soda, then." David looked at her, looking more small and nervous every minute. "Say something, Sarah. I said I like you, and you haven't said anything."

"I like you, too."

As soon as the words came out of her mouth, she realized it was true. She didn't like David the way that Natalie liked Simon, or Brynn liked Darren, or whoever. She didn't get all googly-eyed at the mention of his name or feel like writing their names together on her notebooks with lots of hearts and flowers and doves all around them. (Actually, that thought made her fairly sick.) But she liked talking to him, and she liked being around him more than she'd ever liked being around any boy before. When she was with David, he made her laugh so hard the rest of the world seemed to fade into the background. Was that what it was like to *like-like* someone? Was it possible that you could just be yourself and have fun with someone?

David's face had broken into a huge smile. "Awesome," he said. "It's going to be great, Sars. I can't wait." They had reached the mess hall, and he reached out and patted her arm before he walked off to join his table. "See you tomorrow."

"See you tomorrow," Sarah echoed. She wasn't sure what had just happened there, but just like the night before, she couldn't stop smiling.

▲ ▲ ▲

A couple of days later, Sarah was back in left field. Maybe she was beginning to lose it a little, because she was actually starting to *like* this position now. It was quiet, sure, but she had good company, and she'd more than proven that she was capable of holding her own out here. What had started out as a terrible position had turned out to be for the best.

Too bad Abby still looked like she'd sucked on a lemon every time Sarah did something that wasn't totally incompetent. In fact, Sarah was beginning to get the feeling that her playing well was making Abby *meaner* to her, not nicer. But why would that be? Was Abby really jealous? *If so, she needs to get over it,* Sarah thought. *She gave me enough attitude for messing up. How can she give me attitude for succeeding, too?*

Meanwhile, David had come to the game that morning with eyes and mouths drawn on his hands with ballpoint pen. Between plays, he was putting on a puppet show for Sarah about two girls named Sue and Annie who seemed to keep fighting over their softball game.

As the last inning wound up, David pulled up some grass and dandelions and piled it on top of his left hand. "Oh, Annie," he said in a ridiculously high voice (Sarah figured that was what all boys thought girls sounded like), "are you sure you're jealous of my batting skills, and not my long, lustrous hair?"

Sarah cracked up as Abby struck out the final Panther, and the game ended with their win, 8-4. David walked over to her and continued with "Sue's" monologue: "It's not easy being this beautiful, Annie. Every morning I have to wake up super-early to apply a fertilizer and wash all the ants and caterpillars out…"

"Caterpillars!" Sarah shrieked, laughing. "That's terrible. Can you imagine having a caterpillar in your hair?"

"No." David smiled. "But if *you'd* like to try it, I'm sure it can be arranged…"

"Don't you dare!" Sarah cried. "Remember, I know where you live. And we still have plenty of balloons we can fill up if we need to get you back for any reason."

"You wouldn't."

"I would."

"You wouldn't."

"I have, and I would do it again. And get all my friends in on it."

"Well, there's no *way* I'd let you go a second time. Just keep that in mind."

"Oh, you and your empty threats."

"Hey." Sarah looked up, startled, at the new voice. Jenna was standing before them, stone-faced and angry-looking. Sarah felt a sudden panic—she and David hadn't really waited for Jenna after the last couple of games. Could she be mad? She sure *looked* mad.

"Hey," Sarah replied hesitantly.

Jenna looked over at David. "Sarah, can I speak to you alone, for a minute?"

Sarah felt a chill of panic as she followed Jenna's gaze back to David's confused face. "Uh . . . sure." *Why?* Jenna had never spoken to Sarah that formally before. Her serious expression, combined with this sudden Miss Manners business, made Sarah think that something was definitely up.

Jenna didn't reply, she just led the way away from David and a little ways into the woods. She walked for a few minutes and then stopped in a small clearing, turning to face Sarah. Again, Sarah was stunned by how serious and upset she looked. *What did I do?* she thought, panicking.

Jenna looked past Sarah, at a branch beyond her head. She seemed to be on autopilot as she began. "I heard about you and David."

Sarah frowned. "*What* about me and David?"

Jenna pulled her gaze to Sarah's eyes and made an annoyed face. "What do you *think*, about you and David? I heard that you're a couple now. I heard that you're going to the social together."

"Yeah?" Sarah asked. "Well, yeah, I guess so. We're not a *couple*. But he asked me to go to the social with him, and I said yes."

Jenna nodded slowly, then narrowed her eyes. "I can't believe you would do that to me."

"Do *what* to you?" Sarah blurted in surprise. *What is she talking about? What does David have to do with her?*

"*What* to me?" Jenna rolled her eyes. "Sarah, everybody *knows* I have a huge crush on David. Why do you think I was hanging out with him at the beginning of sports? Why do you think I introduced you to him?"

Sarah couldn't believe her ears. Not only did staunchly antiboy Jenna have a crush, but it was on . . . *David?* "You said he was your brother's friend!" Sarah cried. "I figured he knows Adam and of course Adam knows you. So that made you guys friends. *Just* friends," she added hastily. "I had no idea that you liked him!"

Jenna shook her head, her braid *fwapping* against her shoulder. "No, Sarah. I was hanging out with him because I like him. And I was going to ask him to the social tomorrow . . . before *you* screwed it up."

Sarah couldn't believe Jenna was talking to her like this. *Boys!* It seemed like they were destroying all of her friendships in one way or another. A week ago she would have laughed it off and told Jenna she was welcome to David. But now . . . now she knew she really liked him. What were the chances of two friends liking the same guy at the same time? *I hope this never happens to me again,* Sarah thought sadly.

"What do you want me to do?" she asked. "*He* asked me. And I'm really sorry you didn't get a chance to ask him."

Jenna wouldn't look at her. She stared at the ground. "Too little, too late, Sars," she said quietly. "He's the only boy I've ever liked. And as long as you guys are going to the social . . . I can't just pretend it's okay with me. I'm sorry." She turned suddenly and stalked off down the path. Sarah was left in stunned silence.

What just happened there? Did I just lose a friend over a boy? Sarah heard Jenna stomp down the path, and she replayed their conversation in her mind. *Jenna's been my friend forever,* she mused. *I can't lose a friend over a stupid boy. Especially not a friend who stands up for you and pays attention to you and makes you feel better when you're down.*

She turned and started walking back to the mess hall. She liked David a *lot* . . . but she knew what she had to do.

ELEVEN

"It's so cool that you have a date now, Sars! We can all get ready together . . . and all dance near each other . . . it will be so cool with all of us together!" Brynn beamed at Sarah in the flickering firelight. Sarah felt her heart sink for the hundredth time that evening.

"Sure," she replied unenthusiastically. "Great."

Campfire tonight was just *too* depressing. It didn't help that Sarah had spent the whole day trying to come up with a solution to the Jenna/David problem and had come up with nothing. She was beginning to think there *was* no solution . . . except the obvious.

It's unfair of Jenna to ask this of me, she mused, watching Jenna joke with Jessie and Alyssa across the fire circle. *It's not my fault David likes me, and I like him. But . . .* But Jenna was a long-term friend. David was just a boy. And as much as she liked him, she would do anything to hang on to her friends—especially now, with Abby bad-mouthing her to who-knows-who, and Alex, Valerie, Brynn, and Grace all boy-crazy and social-obsessed.

I need all the friends I can get right now.

Sarah heard a crunching in the leaves on the ground and turned to see David approaching her with a little square of paper. Alex spotted him before he got to her and let out a quiet little "*Wooo*, Sarah! Here he comes!" Sarah just turned and rolled her eyes at her. No matter how great the boy was . . . there was just no excuse to act like *that*.

"Hey!" David greeted her cheerily, holding out the little piece of white paper, which Sarah now saw was a napkin folded into the shape of a frog, with eyes and everything. "I made this for you at dinner. It took me so long, I missed out on the Jell-O. But then I saw it was green, so I didn't mind."

"Green's gross," Sarah agreed. They had so much in common.

"Word," said David.

Sarah took the little frog and turned it over in her hand. It had tiny little arms and legs, and even a smiling red mouth drawn in dry-erase marker that David must have borrowed from the menu board. Looking at it made her feel bad, knowing what she was about to say. "Listen," she said quietly, "can we talk? I need to tell you something."

"Sure thing," agreed David.

Sarah stood up. "How about over by the pagoda?"

David shrugged. "Okay."

Sarah shuffled slowly over to the pagoda. *Maybe if I go slowly enough, I'll never have to tell him*, she thought. But that was silly. No matter how slow she walked, the social would come eventually, and then she would have to say something to David or lose Jenna as a friend. There was just no getting around this.

Sarah stopped in front of the pagoda and turned to David. "Listen," she said, "I've been thinking a lot."

David nodded. "Me too!" he said. "About Spider-Man."

Sarah shook her head. "No. Not about Spider-Man."

David nodded more furiously. "Oh yes! Like, can Spider-Man swim? And if so, can he throw nets in the water? Can he catch fish with his nets? Hmmmm . . ."

Sarah shook her head more furiously. "NO! *I* have not been thinking about Spider-Man. It's great that you have. But I haven't. I've been thinking about . . . the social. And us, going together."

David raised an eyebrow. "Are you thinking we should wear matching outfits? Because if that's what you're thinking, right now, that's *totally* amazing . . ."

"NO!" cried Sarah. "David, be serious! I was thinking about *us* going to the dance together. And I decided . . ." She took a deep breath. David was listening carefully now, and he looked a little nervous, like he sensed what she was about to say. *Is that why he kept interrupting?* She wondered. *Because he knows what I'm getting at?* Sarah sighed. If that was what he was doing, that made her heart hurt more than the little napkin-frog she was now clutching in her left hand.

" . . . I decided we shouldn't go together."

Sarah almost couldn't look at David as she said it, but she had to. She watched his eyes go through a range of emotions: surprise, then recognition, then hurt. She felt her heart catch. He turned away from her before she could see any more.

"Are you serious?" he asked.

Sarah forced herself to nod. "I am. Yeah."

David shook his head. "Why?" he asked. "I thought we made a good team."

I can't do this, Sarah thought. *I don't know what to say. This feels too terrible.*

"I don't know why," she said softly.

David looked startled. "There must be a *why*," he said. "You don't just unaccept someone's dance invitation without a reason. So why?"

Sarah looked at him for a moment. *I have to lie. He'll never let it go if I don't.* "I just don't like you that way," she said very quietly.

But it was loud enough for David to hear. She saw the surprise in his eyes again, and then even more hurt. "You don't, huh," he murmured.

"I don't," Sarah confirmed. She looked away—she couldn't look him in the eye anymore. *Why does this hurt so much?* she wondered. *It took me so long to even figure out that I liked him!*

She heard David take a deep breath, still too scared to look at him. "Okay," he said. And then she heard footsteps walking back to the campfire.

When Sarah looked back up, David was gone. And being alone had never felt quite so lonely.

The next morning, Sarah stood in left field feeling

ready to drop. She'd barely slept at all the night before. Each time she started to relax, she'd picture David's hurt face as she told him she didn't like him "that way." And no matter how many times she pictured his expression, it hurt her to see just as much as it had the first time. *I'm a monster,* she thought. *And worse than that, I'm a liar. I do like him that way! I'm just hurting him to make Jenna feel better.*

Now, David stood a few yards away, but he might as well have been on Mars for all the attention he was paying to Sarah. He stared straight ahead, watching the game, not interacting with her or any other player. He was like the DaveBot 2000. All the human things that made David David seemed to have been washed away.

Since David was ignoring her, Sarah forced herself to concentrate on the game. She was playing better than ever. She hit a home run in the third inning, bringing in three points. She'd caught two fly balls so far. For the first time, it seemed like her teammates were cheering for *her* more than they cheered for Abby. In spite of everything that was going on with David, that was a great feeling.

Now a girl named Julie was up at bat. She usually hit pop flies, so Sarah readied herself. There was a boy on second who kept running up, like he was going to steal a base. Abby kept turning around to toss the ball to second, bringing him back to base.

Finally, Abby pitched the ball to Julie. Strike one. Sarah had to admit it: Abby was a great pitcher. She never lost her concentration, something Sarah herself could stand to work on.

Abby pitched a second time. Julie swung the bat a second too late: strike two. Sarah heard murmurs running through the other team. It was the top of the ninth inning, and the Tigers were leading, 4-3.

Abby pitched for a third time. Julie watched the ball come, and then swung the bat with a resounding *crack*. The ball was flying toward third base. The third baseman, Jimmy, reached for it, but it barely brushed the top of his glove and kept going, bouncing once on the ground. Without thinking, Sarah started booking toward it. She held out her glove and moved faster than she'd ever moved. *There's no way I'll get it*, the rational part of her mind was saying as she ran wildly for the ball. But the other part, the athlete part, was saying, *Just try*.

Sarah could hear her teammates cheering as she flew after the ball. And then, before she could think it through, she was there—and the ball landed in her glove. Moving on instinct, Sarah kept running for third base rather than taking the risk of throwing it. She was only a few yards away. She stomped on third base with the ball in her hand a split second before the base-stealer-wannabe made contact with it. Then she looked to second: Julie had run for it, but she wasn't there yet. As fast as she could, Sarah flung the ball toward the second baseman, who caught it just before Julie slid into the base.

"What an amazing double play!" Kimberly shouted, beaming at Sarah. "That's three outs, game over! Great job, Sarah!"

Sarah was hunched over third base now, trying to catch her breath. She stumbled and realized that the ankle she'd injured during the drills was throbbing again—she'd reinjured it somehow. But the pain was almost lost in the wave of hugs and cheering from her teammates. Within seconds, she was surrounded.

"That was *amazing*, Sarah!" Lily cried.

"You're so awesome!" shouted Gillian, almost suffocating Sarah in a bear-hug.

"You're the star of the team!" said Jimmy.

Teammate after teammate came up to slap Sarah five, hug her, or offer congratulations. They were making up cheers with her name in them and joking with one another about how Sarah had hidden her talents with her disastrous drill performance. Sarah was so happy, she felt like she might burst. *This is what I've wanted this whole time,* she thought. *An amazing play. Everyone's impressed. Even Abby has to admit I'm a great athlete—just like her. And then maybe she'll drop the attitude.*

But where *was* Abby? The whole rest of the team was with Sarah—even David, who'd muttered a quick, "Nice play," before disappearing back into the crowd. Abby, the captain, was nowhere to be seen. Then suddenly Sarah spotted her—across the field, talking to a girl from the other team. Sarah felt her ears burning. Her ankle throbbed, and her eyelids were heavy with lack of sleep. *What is she* doing? she wondered. *The whole team's over here congratulating me, but she's too jealous to even do that. What kind of team captain is she?*

Kimberly and Keith came by to remind the Tigers that the game was over, and if they didn't head for the mess hall soon, they'd miss lunch. Slowly, the team members dispersed and headed toward the mess hall. Sarah limped along behind them, her ankle throbbing with every step. *I'm sick of this,* she fumed. *I'm sick of Abby and her stuck-up attitude.*

She saw Abby a few feet ahead in the crowd, her hot pink T-shirt standing out in the midday heat. Before she could stop herself, Sarah reached out and grabbed a handful of that T-shirt. Abby turned around and looked at her in surprise.

"We have to talk," said Sarah.

chapter
TWELVE

Abby narrowed her eyes at Sarah. She looked surprised that Sarah was confronting her, and also a little annoyed. "Fine," she said shortly, and followed Sarah over to a cluster of trees to the right of the mess hall.

When they stopped, Sarah felt so mad that she thought she might explode. "What's *up* with you?" she demanded loudly. Abby looked surprised, but Sarah kept going. "Did you *see* the play I made just now? Did you even *see* it?"

"I saw it," Abby replied coolly, folding her arms in front of her chest.

Sarah was so frustrated she started to sputter. "You—well—okay—I mean—"

"It was a good play, Sarah," Abby went on, just as cool. "I was impressed. Is that what you wanted to hear?"

Sarah rolled her eyes. "You think?" she cried sarcastically. "You're the team *captain*, Abby. And somehow you have lots of praise for everybody *but* me."

Abby shook her head. "I've praised you, Sarah.

Maybe not as much as you wanted to be praised."

"That's not it!" Sarah shouted, really getting annoyed now. Why couldn't Abby see it? "You're rude to me out there, Abby. You're mean when I play badly, and even meaner when I play well. It's like I'm not *good* enough to be on the team with you."

Abby looked at Sarah skeptically, not saying anything.

"Do you think you're too *cool* for me since you're this big jock at school, or something?" Abby looked a little surprised, but Sarah went on. "Because that's not right! This is Camp Lakeview, Abby, not Winthrop Middle School. And I can be whoever I want here! And I'm a good athlete."

Abby frowned, shaking her head in disbelief. "You think *I'm* the one with the attitude?" she asked. "You think *I'm* the one who thinks I'm too good for you?"

"Yes!" Sarah shouted. *She doesn't think—she can't seriously mean—*

"*You're* the stuck-up one, Sarah!" Abby yelled, her eyes blazing. "At school, you barely even talk to anyone except the other brainiacs, like Diane and them."

Sarah's mouth dropped open. "But I—"

"Here at camp, you act like you're Miss Queen Bee because you've been here before. You don't share any of your friends with me, and you don't include me in anything you do."

Sarah just stood there, too surprised to speak. *Miss Queen Bee? Me?!* She remembered speaking sharply to Abby about the prank war, and it was true, she'd never gone out of the way to invite Abby to anything she was doing with the gang. But that was because Abby had been so stand-offish, she didn't think she'd want to come with them! *But did she act standoffish so I didn't invite her, or did I not invite her so she started to act standoffish?* Sarah gasped. All this time, she'd thought it was Abby taking an attitude with her—what if she'd been the first to throw out signs of attitude? *It must have been hard for Abby, coming alone to a new camp. And the first day, I acted disappointed to see her—because she was ruining my private place.*

But there was more. "That doesn't explain the way you act in softball," Sarah insisted. "You were mad at me when I played bad, but then you seemed even madder when I played well."

Abby rolled her eyes. "Think about it, Sarah. Sports are really important to me. Everyone said you were this great player. But you and that David kid, you were always goofing off and making jokes. I took the team seriously, so that annoyed me."

"Oh—okay," Sarah said slowly, trying to absorb all of this new information. "But—I mean, I really wasn't playing badly on purpose. And that doesn't explain why you didn't chill out when I started playing well."

Abby sighed. "Sarah, like I said, sports are really important to me. The teams I play on at school are really important to me."

Sarah nodded. "Yeah?"

"When I saw what a great player you are, I just felt—*duped*. Like you've been keeping this a secret for who knows how long. Why didn't you ever join any teams back home?"

Sarah shrugged. "I dunno." *I was scared.*

Abby looked down at her feet, then back at Sarah. "I figured you thought you were too good for those teams. Like you wouldn't have enough smart kids to talk to. When I saw how well you played out there—I thought, *This girl must really not want to hang around me.* Why hadn't I ever seen you play like that? Why aren't we friends?"

Sarah looked at Abby in amazement. "I dunno," she said honestly. "I've wondered the same thing. I think you're a great athlete, Abby, and I haven't been avoiding you. I just—I wish I could be more like you. I don't know why I don't go out for the teams at home. Maybe I just don't want the added pressure, or maybe I'm afraid I wouldn't make it in the first place. But I definitely don't think I'm *better* than you. I'm just some shy girl with her nose in a book, and camp is my chance to be different."

Abby nodded, looking surprised. "I guess—I haven't been fair to you," she admitted.

"But I haven't been fair to you either," Sarah said. "I've been so busy competing with you, I forgot that the reason we compete is we both want the same things. We have a lot in common."

"Yeah," agreed Abby.

"Look," said Sarah, "I'm not going to promise some fairy-tale transformation, like we'll be best friends from now on or whatever. But I'll try to be nicer to you if you'll do the same."

Abby nodded. "That sounds like a deal."

Sarah smiled. "And maybe I'll go out for some team next year."

"Awesome." Abby had a nice smile, Sarah realized. Slowly, they began walking toward the mess hall, where lunch was just beginning. "Hey," Abby said suddenly, "I forgot to tell you something."

"What?"

Abby turned around and punched Sarah hard in the shoulder, a big smile on her face. "Kick-butt play, Tiger!"

Sarah stood in surprise for a second, then laughed and rubbed her arm. "Thanks," she said. "Thanks a lot."

Dinner that night was so much better than the other dinners had been, and Sarah wondered whether anyone even noticed besides her and Abby.

"Sarah made this *amazing* double play today in softball," Abby told the bunkmates. "It was like, impossible. She bent time and space."

Sarah laughed. "Come on! It wasn't that amazing. Besides, we'd never be doing as well as we are if it weren't for your pitching. You're so steady, it's incredible."

Gaby looked from Abby to Sarah and back again. "Are you guys okay? Was there some big lovefest I wasn't invited to?"

Sarah chuckled and shook her head. "Just mutual appreciation, Gaby." She looked at Abby and winked. "Something only true athletes understand."

"Hey!" Brynn said, turning to Sarah. "I heard you're not going to the dance with David anymore. Why not?"

Sarah shrugged, feeling uncomfortable. "I don't know. I just decided . . . I don't like him that way."

"*Really?*" asked Abby incredulously. "But you guys talk all the time in softball. You seem to get along really well."

Sarah tried to concentrate on her bug juice. "Getting along isn't everything," she said. "I just . . . didn't feel ready for the whole romantic thing. You know."

Alex shrugged. "I guess. Anyway, it's no big deal, Sars. The rest of the social committee didn't seem very impressed with our ideas."

Sarah paused in mid-sip. "Really?"

Alex nodded. "Really. They kept vetoing all of our ideas to make the dance more romantic—more slow music, softer lighting, whatever. They said it would be too uncomfortable for the younger kids."

And for me, thought Sarah. "Seriously?"

Grace nodded. "Yeah. And here it is just a couple of days till the dance, and I don't have a date, Alex doesn't have a date—"

Alex broke out laughing. "Hey, hey, hey! I still have time!"

Grace laughed. "Okay, whatever, Alex. The point is, I think only Brynn and Gaby have dates, right? Oh and I guess Priya and Jordan, and Nat and Simon. But you knew that. And anyway, as Priya always says—she and Jordan are—"

"*Just friends*," all the bunkmates chorused in unison.

Brynn and Gaby nodded as the other girls looked at each other and shrugged.

"It looks like most of us will be going stag," Grace said. "So it'll be more like last year than we expected."

Sarah grinned. "Awesome," she said. "Circle dancing, here we come!"

As dessert was finishing up—green Jell-O, which, sadly, made Sarah think of David—Jenna strolled over with a friendly smile. "Hey, guys," she greeted the table. Then she turned to Sarah. "Can I talk to you for a minute?"

"Sure." Sarah got up and followed Jenna over to the mess-hall entrance, which was a little ways off from the rest of the tables. "What's up?"

"I heard you told David that you won't go to the dance with him."

Sarah cringed. She knew it should make her feel better that Jenna knew—it meant that Jenna would stop being mad at her and everything would go back to normal. But even the mention of David's name made Sarah feel awful. She carried his napkin-frog in her shorts pocket—not that she would tell anyone about that. "Yeah," Sarah said, not quite sure how to proceed. "So . . ."

"I just wanted to say thanks for respecting my feelings," said Jenna, looking a little sheepish. "I mean, I'm glad you didn't like him that way. I'm *not* sorry I told you what I told you. It would have been really weird for me, hanging out with the two of you as a couple! But I'm sorry if . . . you know . . . feelings got hurt. Or whatever." Now, for the first time, she looked Sarah in the eye. "I think you're a really great friend, Sars."

Sarah didn't know what to say. "Thanks." She wondered if Jenna expected her to say it back. The thing was, a few days ago, Sarah *would* have said Jenna was a great friend—but lately, when she thought of Jenna, all she thought about was David's hurt face when she told him she didn't like him that way. So she stayed quiet, fiddling with the frog in her pocket.

"Okay," said Jenna finally. "Well, I just wanted you

to know that."

Slowly they made their way back to their tables. Sarah sighed, thinking over the day. *I made up with Abby. I found my inner athlete. Jenna and I are cool, and the dance thing seems to be going my way.* She paused before her table, looking around at her friends. *So why am I not happy?*

"Definitely the purple eye shadow," Brynn was saying as she applied quick brushstrokes to Sarah's eyelids. "*Definitely* the purple. Sarah, this looks gorgeous on you. It makes your eyes look huge."

Sarah blinked, having trouble sitting still. "Freakishly huge?" she asked nervously. "Like big fish eyes?"

Brynn sighed and looked down at Sarah. "*Good* huge, Sarah. Wait till you see how gorgeous you look. It's like a whole new you."

Becky walked over to survey Sarah's makeover. Brynn had offered to use the "incredible makeup skills" she'd picked up in drama to make Sarah gorgeous for the dance. Sarah wasn't sure why she'd submitted to it—she felt very exposed, very naked without her Red Sox hat. And having makeup put on one's face was a weird, strangely awkward experience. Sarah was afraid she'd get a pencil in the eye or some lashes pulled out with Brynn's lash curler, but so far, so good. Of course, she hadn't seen herself yet.

"Wow, Sarah," Becky breathed. "You look *so*

awesome, girl. I didn't realize you had such long eyelashes."

Sarah shrugged—or shrugged as much as she could without getting an eye-shadow brush in the eye. "Neither did I."

"Wow, Sarah," Abby imitated Becky, sweeping up out of nowhere, "that makeup really does incredible things for you. I never noticed that third eye on the side of your face, or the mole with the hair growing out of it—"

"Stop it!" Brynn cried as Sarah laughed. "She's totally making that stuff up, Sars. I don't know what's wrong with her."

"Wouldn't it be great if you actually *did* draw in an extra eye with makeup?" Abby asked. "How funny would that be? I'm *totally* borrowing someone's eyeliner."

"Abby, you're nuts!" Grace shrieked. "I can't believe how crazy you are. I can't believe I didn't notice it before."

Abby raised an eyebrow. "I keep it well-hidden," she admitted. "But once you get to know me—watch out!"

"Okay," Brynn was saying, sweeping a rose-colored lip gloss over Sarah's lips. "I think you're done, Sars. Just let me add one coat of mascara . . ."

Sarah tried not to blink as Brynn coated her lashes with the cold liquid.

Brynn stood back to survey her work. "*Amazing!*" she cried. "You are so gorgeous. You're going to blow away all the guys at the social."

"Poor David will pee his pants," Alex added.

Sarah's heart sunk at the mention of David's name. A few days had passed since she'd told him she wouldn't go with him, and she kept expecting it to hurt less, but so far, no luck. Bunk 4E still hadn't retaliated for the water-balloon prank, and she couldn't help wondering whether she was part of the reason. She didn't want David to pee his pants at the sight of her. In fact, she didn't want to think about David being there, at all.

"Let me see," she said, standing up from Grace's bunk and walking into the bathroom to look at herself in the mirror. When she approached it, a person she'd never seen before waited for her on the other side. Was that *her*? Sarah's light brown hair was styled in gentle waves that curled around her face and rested gently on her pink peasant top. And Brynn was right, the purple eye shadow made her hazel eyes look wide and sparkly. Her cheeks were just slightly rosy with pink blush, and her lips shone with a soft rose sheen. It was her—there was no denying that she was looking at Sarah—but she was *pretty*. So pretty, she was almost afraid to touch her face, or it would wear off.

"You like it?" Brynn asked, appearing behind her in the mirror.

"Like it?" Sarah whirled around and engulfed Brynn in a huge hug. "God, Brynn, thank you! I don't know what you did, but I love it."

"Let's go, girls!" Valerie called, popping into the bathroom. "We're supposed to meet 4A over by the oak tree in three minutes!"

Everyone exploded into motion, running in circles around the bathroom and cubbies, doing last-minute primping. Finally they began filing out the door and down to the oak tree. The night air was cool and refreshing, and Sarah realized that she would have been tingling with excitement, if only she were going with David. Who knew that having a date to the social would *ever* sound like a good idea?

The girls from 4A poured out of the cabin in a cloud of glitter and perfume. They all looked amazing, in stylish tops and jeans and dangly earrings. Sarah couldn't believe these were her everyday friends. They all looked like models on their way to a catalog shoot.

"You look gorgeous!" Natalie gushed to Sarah. "Who did your makeup? I never realized you have such pretty eyes!"

"They're always hidden under that baseball cap," agreed Alex, giving Sarah's arm a gentle squeeze.

"Maybe I won't wear my Red Sox hat *every* day from now on," Sarah allowed. "But when I feel the need, I'm supporting my team. Some things are more important than beauty."

"I hear that," Abby called.

Everybody was in a great mood on the walk to the rec hall, gossiping and chatting and making silly jokes about nothing. When they walked inside the hall, everybody gasped. It looked amazing. The theme for the dance was "Starry Nights," and the gym was decorated with hundreds of twinkling white lights, dark blue crepe paper, and a huge papier-mâché moon. *The fourth-division girls on social committee may not have gotten everything they wanted, but they definitely did a great job*, Sarah thought.

The DJ was already playing great dance music, so they all jumped onto the dance floor and started dancing in a big circle. The dance floor was already littered with other circles—the third-division girls and a group of

CITs. Natalie, Brynn, Priya, and Gaby all went in search of their dates (Priya still insisting Jordon wasn't a "date"), but everyone else hung together and danced like crazy. Soon, the other girls came back with Simon, Darren, and Gaby's date, a tall, skinny boy named Matt. Sarah was dancing so hard, she was almost out of breath.

But then she looked up and saw some boys from 4E standing against the wall across the room. And there he was: David. Sarah's heart sunk. She wondered what it would have been like if she'd gone with him—would he have come and danced in their circle, too? Or would she be standing with him against the wall, watching her friends dance and wishing she could be with them? He looked really great in a pale yellow plaid shirt that brought out his green eyes. Sarah wondered if the boys primped as much for these dances as the girls did. *Doubt it,* she figured. *But he still looks great.*

They'd been dancing for a while now, and suddenly Abby appeared beside her, mopping off her brow. "I'm thirsty!" she yelled to Sarah over the music. "Wanna get something to drink?"

"Sure!" Sarah yelled. She turned to Alyssa, who was dancing beside her. "We'll be right back," she explained. Then she followed Abby off the dance floor and over to the refreshments. Sarah grabbed a Coke, while Abby took a glass of punch. Sarah leaned against the table, her eyes helplessly drawn to the spot where David stood with his friends. He would laugh and joke with them, but his eyes kept going back to the spot where the fourth-division girls were dancing. *He's looking for me,* Sarah realized.

"He's totally into you," Abby said suddenly, reading

her mind. Sarah turned around and found Abby looking at her sympathetically.

"I know," Sarah said quietly. "And I like him, too, but Jenna would hate me forever if we got together."

Abby made a *what?!* face. "Why would she hate you?"

"Because she likes him, too, and she thinks it would be hard to be friends with us if we got together." Even as she said it, Sarah knew it was going to sound silly to Abby. It sounded silly to her, too, put like that. And sure enough, when she turned back to Abby, Abby was wearing a skeptical expression. She looked back at David, who was searching the fourth-division girls again.

"Sometimes you have to fight for the things you want," Abby told her with a wink, and then walked back to dance with their bunkmates again. Sarah was left alone by the refreshments table. She had butterflies in her stomach. The Sarah that she was at home would probably ignore that funny feeling in her stomach and go back to dancing, but there was only one Sarah now, and she was trying to be braver.

The song ended, and Sarah headed back to the fourth-division girls. But she wasn't going back to dance. She touched Jenna lightly on the shoulder. "Come outside with me?" she asked. Jenna looked puzzled, but she stopped dancing and followed Sarah out of the gym. The cool air felt wonderful after all that dancing. Sarah leaned against a railing and turned to face her friend. "I need to tell you something," she began.

Jenna looked skeptical. "Okay."

Sarah took a deep breath. "I told David I wouldn't

go with him tonight because I didn't want to lose you as a friend, but the truth is I really do like him, and I think he likes me. And you're one of my favorite people, Jenna, and a great friend, but it's not fair of you to ask me to stay away from him to make you feel better. And I think I'm going to ask him to dance."

Sarah carefully watched Jenna's face when she finished. For a moment, Jenna looked completely furious. *Oh god, I've done it, I've really lost her as a friend*, Sarah thought. But then Jenna looked back through the gym windows. And there, she saw David, watching them talk from inside the gym. *He must have seen us leave*, Sarah realized. Jenna's face fell, and she sighed, then shook her head.

"Okay," she said. She looked away, into the woods. "I get it, Sars. He really likes you. Okay."

Sarah leaned over and gave her friend a huge hug. Jenna didn't respond, but then she didn't squirm away, either. Sarah felt confident that she would come around. "Thank you," she whispered. Then she let go, caught David's eye, and walked quickly through the gym door.

"Hey," she said softly, walking up to David.

"Hey yourself," he replied. "You, um . . . you look great."

Sarah smiled. "So do you." She paused and leaned against the wall. "So . . . about that favor I owe you, since you let me go that night . . ."

David nodded. "Yeah, I guess you still owe me that."

Sarah nodded. "What if I admitted something to you? Would that make us even?"

David looked surprised. "That depends on what

that something is."

Sarah took a deep breath and looked him in the eye. "The something is that . . . what I told you before? About not liking you in *that way?*"

"Oh, yeah," David murmured. "I sort of remember something like that."

Sarah sighed. "What if I told you . . . it was all a lie? And that I really do like you *that way*, a whole lot. And . . . I'm really, *really* sorry."

David looked at her, considering. "Huh," he muttered. "Well . . ." He looked out the window at the stars, and stroked his chin. "I don't think it would make us *even*," he said finally. "But it might make us closer to even."

Sarah smiled and grabbed his arm. "Come dance with me and my friends?" she asked.

David laughed and eagerly followed. "I thought you'd never ask."

The circle was just as Sarah had left it, except that Jenna wasn't back yet. Sarah squeezed in and made room for David and herself. She caught Abby's eye on the other side of the circle and winked. Abby winked back immediately.

One of Sarah's favorite songs started to play, and she felt her body responding to the music before she even had time to think about it—kind of like how she felt when she was playing sports. She looked at the smiling faces of her friends as they all danced to the music and grinned. She knew that whoever Sarah was from this point on—bookish, a jock, a romantic, whatever—she was going to be a whole lot happier.

Turn the page for a sneak preview of

camp CONFIDENTIAL

Second Summer

Best (Boy)friend
Forever

available soon!

chapter ONE

Hey, Sam-bone!

Sorry I haven't written more, li'l bro. But you know how much I hate to sit still. And there's so much to do at Camp Lakeview. B-Ball. Swimming in the lake. Soccer. Moonlit hikes. And some pretty chilly pranks have been played already this summer.

I had this tree-climbing contest with Jordan, and I almost fell. Don't tell Mom!! I won, so it's all good. Except, the next day, Jordan beat me in this game we invented. Bike-broom polo. I'll teach it to you when I get home. You'll go ape over it.

With the tree and the polo included, that makes the overall score so far for the summer: Priya 43-Jordan 41. I so rule! Except that, okay, Jordan has been ahead of me a couple times since we started our Year 2 Camp Lakeview Who's-the-Most-Extreme Challenge. He's like you. Fearless. And stupid. (Hee-hee.) Which means that, also, like you, he's already had three broken bones in his life. And, yes, I know I've had two in my twelve years on the planet, plus that thing that time with my tooth. What is it that Dad says? The thrill of victory, the agony of defeat? I still say the thrill was worth the agony of the teeth. 'Cause I did conquer that empty swimming pool with my skateboard. You know it.

How're you? How's the all-star team? Getting to play at D-land, that so rocks. I miss you, but hanging with Jordan helps, because we do a lot of the same stuff the two of us do. He's my Summer Sam, minus a lot of the annoying little brother stuff. (Hee-HAW!) Really, Jordan's the best friend EVER!!! But you're the best bro.

I can't wait until Friday. That's when the whole fourth division is heading off for our long weekend—4 days!!!—in Washington, D.C. Jordan and I have already made a zillion plans. We're definitely going to do this thing called the Sites on Bikes. That's where you bike around all the monuments. (Do you think it's possible to scale the Washington Monument? Because how amazing would it be to rappel down that thing? Just kidding. Mostly. I mean it would be fun, but even I'm not that deranged.) And we're going to spend one whole day in the National Air and Space Museum. Did I ever tell you Jordan's an astro-nut, just like me?

Gotta go. Time for dinner. And that means time for barf on a bun. Otherwise known as Sloppy Joe Surprise.

Bye!

Your favorite (and, okay, only) sister,

Priya

▲ ▲ ▲

"Bat!" Priya Shah called out. The bandanna tied around her eyes made her blind as a . . . you know.

"Tree!" someone to her left answered.

"Moth!" someone behind her squeaked. She was positive it was Jordan, trying to disguise his voice.

Two other people called out "moth" from somewhere in front of her. She felt kinda sure Grace from her bunk was one of them, because of the Grace-like, but not moth-like, giggling.

Priya spun around, in the direction of the squeaky definitely Jordan voice. "Bat!" she called out again. She got answers of "tree" and "moth" from all around her, along with some more probably Grace giggles. Priya focused on one particular "moth." This time it had been called out in a deep, booming voice. But Priya's best friend couldn't fool her. She'd spent part of every day at Camp Lakeview with Jordan Bryant. And part of almost every day with him last summer. She knew him inside out. They'd even exchanged most embarrassing moments (on a dare). His: calling his second-grade teacher "Mommy" in front of everybody.

Hers: peeing in her pants at Holly Perry's seventh birthday party after proving that she could chug a half gallon of lemonade without taking a breath and then getting really, really involved in a game of hide-and-seek.

"Bat! Bat! Bat!" Priya yelled. Arms outstretched, she stumbled toward the voice calling "moth" that she was sure was Jordan's. *Gotcha*, she thought. Then she launched herself into the darkness and tackled . . . somebody . . . onto the grass. She jerked off her blindfold. Green eyes. Messy longish brown hair. Freckles. Yep, it was Jordan.

"Great echolocation, Priya," Roseanne, the woman in charge of the nature hut, called. "You guys see how the bat located its dinner? When Priya called 'bat,' that was like a bat sending out an ultrasonic beep. And when you guys answered, that was like the bat receiving the echoes from the beeps. That's how bats pinpoint where things are."

"I rule!" Priya shoved her fists into the air.

Jordan climbed to his feet. "Congratulations, bat girl. You just ate a moth."

"So? Good source of protein," Priya told him as she stood up.

"Priya's right," Roseanne agreed. She ran her fingers through her long curly hair, making it even more wild. Priya was glad her own sandy hair was short, short, short. Pretty much nothing she did could mess it up. Roseanne continued, "Insects are high in protein and low in fat and cholesterol. They are really nutritious. I have some chocolate-covered grasshoppers back in the hut if any of you want to try them."

"No, thank you. I'm on a special diet. Nothing that

hops," Grace joked. "I'm really missing the frog legs and kangaroo meat. But I've lost like an eighth of a quarter of a pound already."

Maybe if they're gummy grasshoppers she'll go for it, Priya thought. Grace had a serious gummy bear habit.

"That is completely disgusting. And chocolate does have fat," Chelsea, one of the bunk 4A girls, decreed. She narrowed her eyes at Grace. "You might want to consider cutting out chocolate if you're serious about losing weight."

"But I'm not," Grace answered.

Priya shot Jordan a wicked smile. "I'm thinking three points," she whispered to him. No way would he let a grasshopper into his mouth, even one that was covered in sweet chocolaty goodness. He was the Picky Eater poster boy. Jordan didn't even like the foods he was willing to eat to touch each other. "That would put you one point ahead of me," she added, just to torture him. As if he didn't totally know that already.

"How is that extreme?" Jordan asked. "How is that worthy of the Who's-the-Most-Extreme Challenge?"

"Oh, right." Priya shook her head. "You eat bugs every day. It's not extreme at all."

"You know what would be extreme?" Jordan asked, leaning close to her, his breath hot against her ear. "If you made me kiss someone."

Priya jerked back and stared at her best friend. *Wh-what?*

"Bug juice. I will perish of dehydration if Priya doesn't pass me the bug juice!" Brynn exclaimed.

"Priya!" Sarah, Alex, and Abby called together, with their hands cupped around their mouths.

Priya blinked. "Huh?" She realized that she had frozen, holding her Sloppy Joe halfway to her mouth. She also realized that everyone at her table in the mess hall—which meant every girl in her bunk—was staring at her. "What?" she asked.

Sarah smiled. "Brynn has asked you for the bug juice, like, three times."

"Oh. Sorry." Priya passed the plastic pitcher of bright red bug juice across the table to Brynn.

"I'm going to live!" Brynn cried dramatically, green eyes all twinkly. Brynn pretty much said everything dramatically. She was really into theater. She'd just played Little Orphan Annie in the camp production of the musical. She already had the red hair, but that's not why she got the part. Brynn was really talented. Although sometimes it got annoying when she didn't keep the drama on the stage.

"What were you thinking about, anyway?" Alex asked Priya. "You were totally zonked."

Priya felt her cheeks get hot. She knew her face had to be turning red, even with her tan.

"She's blushing. It has to be good," Gaby observed. "Tell, tell, tell."

Priya took a mega bite of her Joe to give herself time to think. Should she tell them what had really been going through her brain? The girls in her bunk were pretty cool. But she didn't know them that well. Her best friend at camp was Jordan. She spent as much time with him as possible.

But what she'd been thinking about . . . it was nothing she could talk to Jordan about. Because it was *about* Jordan.

"Well?" Gaby prompted as soon as Priya swallowed. The girl could be a little pushy. Geez.

"She doesn't have to tell if she doesn't want to," Alex said, knocking a soccer ball back and forth between her feet under the table. Bunk 4C's own Mia Hamm was the bunk peacekeeper.

"No, it's okay," Priya told her, deciding to go for it. This sitch was probably something she could use the girl POV on. Even back at home, she didn't hang with girls that much. She was on the boys' soccer team, and she did stuff with Sam a lot. Her little brother was only a little more than a year younger than she was, and he liked almost all the same things she did. Meanwhile, her boyfriend was Jordan. At home, at camp . . . at always.

"Well?" Gaby said again, her lower lip sticking out in a pout. She always pouted when she didn't get what she wanted right when she wanted it. That or threw a tantrum.

Priya sucked in a deep breath. But she still didn't feel ready. So she took a long drink of bug juice. Choked on it. Then started to talk. "Um, you know that competition I have with Jordan?"

"As in the competition that has required three visits to Nurse Helen?" Becky, their counselor, asked. It wasn't a question.

"Uh-huh." Priya nodded. "But we aren't doing

anything that might require a nurse anymore. I swear. So, anyway, I was telling him that I'd give him three points if he'd eat a grasshopper—"

"What?" Valerie burst out. Gaby's pout opened up into an O of surprise.

"Roseanne said she had chocolate-covered grass-hoppers in the nature hut," Grace explained. "Priya wasn't just going to catch one in the field and make him eat it with its legs kicking or anything."

"Oh, ew." Abby wrinkled her nose.

"Ew," Candace echoed. Candace repeated things a lot.

"I'm sure they were sterilized or something," Grace reassured Katie. "Roseanne wouldn't offer us food—or whatever you call it—that would send us to the nurse."

"This doesn't have anything to do with the grass-hopper," Priya said quickly. "See, Jordan said something after I gave him the grasshopper challenge. Something, um, weird. I don't know what it means." Her words came out faster and faster. "Maybeitdoesn'tmeananything."

"You should sign up for drama next time," Brynn said loudly and slowly. "You need to do some work on your e-nun-ci-a-tion." She winked.

"So tell us what he said already," Gaby ordered.

Priya reached for her glass of bug juice again, then told herself not to be such a chicken. "He said that if I wanted to give him a really extreme challenge, I should make him to kiss someone."

Sophie, their CIT, put a bowl of sort of old-looking fruit on their table, and lingered, ears wide open.

"Oooob." Grace leaned closer.

"Yeah, *ooooh*," Candace said.

"I need more details," Valerie told Priya. "Was there anyone else in the group when you two were talking about the kissing thing?"

"No," Priya answered. "He didn't exactly whisper it. But he leaned in. He was definitely only talking to me."

"Interesting," Valerie said.

Priya's heart started skipping rope inside her chest. "Interesting? Why? Why interesting?"

"Sounds like he liiiikes you," Sarah said. And Sarah should know. She'd just found out that this guy David liked her.

"Sounds like maybe he even wants to kiss you," Abby added.

"No way. We're buds, compadres, amigos, uh, pals, um . . ." Priya's voice trailed off. She couldn't think of any more words.

"Mates, chums," Grace volunteered as she peeled one of the mushy bananas.

"Jordan's my best friend," Priya told the group, going for the simple truth. "You don't go around kissing your best friend. That's just . . . yuck on a stick."

"But wasn't there that movie with Austin Kutcher and Amanda somebody where they're best friends and then they fall in love?" Abby asked.

"It's Ashton," Alex told her. "Repeat after me. Ashton."

"I just meant that just because he's your friend, it doesn't mean he couldn't end up feeling something else," Abby explained. "Not that I know what I'm talking about. Sports are my life. Not boys."

"You guys, you're freakin' me out. And I was already freaked out because I thought that what Jordan said meant he was ready to jump into the boyfriend/girlfriend thing with some girl. I got the wiggins thinking he wanted to kiss *any* girl. Forget about me!"

"Maybe he was just talking about kissing in a general kind of way," Alex said. "Don't go into a total meltdown."

"Right. You're right. Or, or, maybe Jordan just said the worst thing he could think of," Priya suggested, unable to think about anything but the big stinking mess her best friend had created. "Like that kissing was even worse than eating a grasshopper." Except for that part where his mashed potatoes touching his salad dressing made Jordan go into a minor freak. Eating a grasshopper had to be very, very high on his list of worsts.

"And that was the very worst thing he could come up with?" Valerie shook her head, her cornrows flopping around her face. "That would make him one sick boy. I mean, there are many bad things in the world."

"Would it really be so absolutely, completely terrible to be boyfriend/girlfriend with Jordan?" Sarah asked. "Maybe not the kissing thing. At least not right away." A slight blush crept up her neck and into her cheeks. "I definitely wanted to punch David when I first thought he liked me, but now it's really cool."

"But you guys weren't ever best friends like me and Jordan," Priya answered. "You found out pretty fast that he liked you liked you. And he probably knew from the beginning. Jordan—he's almost like my brother. I've seen him pick his nose, okay?"

"Too much information," Abby cried.

"I didn't need to know that fact," Candace agreed.

"Yeah, I think I'll take myself back to the kitchen now," Sophie said. She gave them a little wave as she hurried away.

"I just couldn't think of him as a boyfriend," Priya said. She let out a long sigh. "Anyway, he was probably just kidding around. Right?"

Nobody answered fast enough for her.

"Right," Priya said, answering her own question.

But not quite convincing herself.